Florence

MEGAN RIX is the winner of the Stockton and Shrewsbury Children's Book Awards, and has been shortlisted for numerous other children's book awards. She lives with her husband by a river in England. When she's not writing, she can be found walking her gorgeous dogs, Bella and Freya, who are often in the river.

Books by Megan Rix

THE BOMBER DOG

ECHO COME HOME

EMMELINE AND THE PLUCKY PUP

THE GREAT ESCAPE

THE GREAT FIRE DOGS

THE HERO PUP

THE PAW HOUSE

THE RUNAWAYS

A SOLDIER'S FRIEND

THE VICTORY DOGS

WINSTON AND THE MARMALADE CAT

www.meganrix.com

Florence
and the
Mischievous
Kitten

megan rix

PUFFIN

PUFFIN BOOKS

UK | USA | Canada | Ireland | Australia
India | New Zealand | South Africa

Puffin Books is part of the Penguin Random House group of companies
whose addresses can be found at global.penguinrandomhouse.com.

www.penguin.co.uk
www.puffin.co.uk
www.ladybird.co.uk

Penguin
Random House
UK

First published 2019

001

Set in 13/20 pt Baskerville MT
Typeset by Jouve (UK), Milton Keynes
Printed and bound in Great Britain by Clays Ltd, Elcograf S.p.A.

A CIP catalogue record for this book is available from the British Library

ISBN: 978-0-241-36912-8

All correspondence to:
Puffin Books
Penguin Random House Children's
80 Strand, London WC2R ORL

Life is a splendid gift – there is
nothing small about it
Florence Nightingale

Prologue

It was late afternoon in the cats' room of number 10 South Street, London. Eight of the nine fluffy Persian cats and kittens were dozing in the golden light of the spring sunshine streaming in through the floor-length window. Some lay on cushions on the floor while others were curled up on the furniture. A big white cat purred sleepily as a maid stroked him. The other maid had nodded off over her knitting and was snoring softly with her mouth open. An elderly lady dressed in black with a delicate lace cap over her greying hair looked over, smiled to herself, and went back to reading *The Times* newspaper as she sipped a cup of tea.

It was at that precise moment that the ninth cat of the household, ten-week-old Scamp, emerged from his favourite hiding place beneath the sofa, wide awake and ready to play. His soft white, black and ginger fur was sticking up in all directions. He tapped one of his front paws on the face of an older fluffy black-and-white cat named Aggy. But Aggy didn't want to play. She stretched out her paws as far as they would go, rolled over on her velvet cushion, curled up in a ball and went back to sleep. Undeterred, Scamp play-stalked Soyer, a nervous grey cat with bright blue eyes who was lying nearby. But Soyer spotted the kitten through half-closed eyes, jumped up and hid under the chair that held the snoozing maid. Scamp patted his paw instead at a ginger cat called Dickens who was snoozing in front of the flickering fire. But Dickens didn't like being disturbed one little bit. He arched his back as he stood up, hissed at the nuisance kitten and then raked at him with his claws.

Determined to find a playmate, Scamp darted out of Dickens's way, leapt over Tom and Topsy, two tabby kittens sharing a cushion, and up on to the arm of the chaise longue. Sleepy Izzy half opened her eyes to watch Scamp run along the squishy fabric towards the writing desk where the elderly lady was reading *The Times*.

'How on earth does Gladstone expect people to survive?' the lady muttered to herself as she turned a page.

The black cat she'd named after the current prime minister looked up at the sound of his name. 'No, not you,' she told the cat with a fond smile. 'You're a good cat. I meant the other Gladstone.'

She lifted the newspaper up to carry on reading, but at that very moment Scamp leapt from the sofa and came crashing into her lap, ripping the paper clean down the middle.

'Well, really, Scamp! How am I supposed to read the newspaper now?' the lady exclaimed as a surprised Scamp jumped down on to the floor, taking a fluttering page with him. He proceeded to roll himself over on the paper until he'd wrapped himself inside it like a caterpillar in a cocoon. 'So that's what you think of the news, is it?' she chuckled as she watched the kitten. He gazed up at her, one huge amber eye peeking through a black patch of fur, the other eye being surrounded by snowy white. 'You're such a funny, mischievous little kitten.'

Scamp rolled out of his newspaper blanket and gave a *miaow*.

Chapter 1

'And will the match trade die?
*   And will the match trade die?*
*   Then thirty thousand working girls*
*   Will know the reason why.'*

Beth joined in the chant as she stared up at the latticed windows of the magnificent Palace of Westminster. Around her, thousands of match-workers shouted and sang the words over and over. The palace contained the Houses of Parliament, but was anyone inside listening?

The march had started from Bow Station at noon and ended here at four. Seven long miles they'd marched and not a sip to drink or a bite to eat all day.

Beth didn't work at the Bryant and May match factory yet, like most of the marchers, because she was only eleven years old. But her sister Iris was twenty-two and had been working at the factory ever since their family had come over from Ireland six years ago. Beth thought about her poor sister having to work there every day, dipping matches in white phosphorous alongside hundreds of other girls and women.

'The walls are grimy and the place stinks!' Iris had told Beth last week. Her Irish accent always became particularly pronounced when she was vexed. 'We can't even leave the phosphorous bench to have a bite to eat without our wages being docked. It's like being in Hell!'

'Don't say that, Iris,' Beth had replied miserably. She didn't want it to be as bad as all that – but she'd been to the factory a few times and knew exactly what her sister meant.

'You'll never believe what Harry the foreman told us,' Iris continued, folding her arms.

'What?'

'The government's decided to put a penny tax on matches.'

'No!'

Iris nodded. 'And whose wages d'you think will be going down because of it? The match-workers, that's whose!'

Beth's mouth fell open in horror. Iris hardly earnt enough money to keep them from starving as it was. This new tax would be a huge blow.

'Well, the match-workers won't stand for it!' Iris said. 'The bosses are giving us the afternoon off next week and we're all going to march on Parliament and tell them it isn't right. There's going to be so many of us Harry said it should be called the Monster March of 1871! Girls from the big factories and small factories will be there as well as the home-workers.'

Home-workers were paid even less than Iris was. Beth knew that everyone in the family, even the smallest children, had to help make the matches just to earn a crust.

Beth handed Iris a bowl of yesterday's cold watery onion soup and half a slice of bread, salvaged from her own ragged school lunch.

'I bet the prime minister's not living on bread and cold slop,' Iris said. 'Oh no!' But she gave her sister a grateful smile all the same.

Beth shook her head. 'And I bet he doesn't live in a room with only a cracked window and black mould growing up the walls, either.'

They both looked up at the tiny window that had one of Beth's drawings wedged over the crack to stop the wind from whistling in. The drawing was of a tree in blossom, but Beth had never felt so aware that there weren't any trees nearby. Just so many people and the slums they called home, all squashed together.

'You'll come with me on the march, won't you, Beth?' Iris said that night as they huddled together, shivering, in their small rickety bed.

'Yes, I'll come,' Beth promised, pulling the covers up round her ears.

But as it turned out Iris couldn't go on the march.

'What is it? What's wrong?' Beth had asked her when they'd woken up just this morning.

Iris's face was red and her cheeks were swollen.

'Oh, Beth, it's agony!' Iris cried. 'I feel like my whole face is on fire and there's hot pokers jabbing at my gums. I can't go to work and I can't go on the march like this. You'll have to go without me.'

'I can't leave you alone,' Beth said. 'Not when you're in so much pain.'

'You must! We have to let the government know the match tax isn't right. People can barely feed themselves as it is. The tax'll send families into the workhouse. Don't worry, the other girls and Harry will look after you.'

'But, Iris . . .'

'Go – go, please. And take Mammy's shawl with you. It'll keep you warm.'

Beth took the woollen shawl from the hook on the wall. It was one of the few belongings they had to remember their parents by.

'I'm sorry there's no food for you,' Iris said. They'd eaten the last of the stale bread yesterday.

'I'm not hungry anyway,' Beth lied as she laced up her boots. 'You stay in bed and rest.'

By the time she left the room Iris had already fallen fast asleep. Beth hoped she'd sleep the rest of the day away and not feel the pain. 'Back soon,' she whispered. Iris didn't stir.

The boots pinched Beth's toes and one of them had a hole in the sole. She hadn't told Iris because she'd only worry and they couldn't afford to buy new ones.

'At least you *have* shoes,' she told herself as she left the house. Most of the other children who went to the ragged school didn't have any shoes at all.

Even before Beth arrived at Bow Station she could hear excited voices. As she turned the corner she saw hundreds of match girls from the Bryant and May factory already at the station along with Harry the foreman. Many of the factory girls were only a year or two older than Beth, but the match home-workers were women of all ages – some were carrying their babies and had small children clinging to their skirts.

'Got any food?' a thin grubby-faced little girl asked her and Beth shook her head. The girl couldn't have been older than three.

'Sorry.'

'Where's Iris?' Harry said when he spotted her. He was rolling up a petition that Beth could see was full of signatures and scrawled initials and Xs.

'She's got a terrible pain in her mouth and her face is all red and swollen,' Beth told him. 'I've come in her place.'

Harry frowned. 'Is it her tooth or her jaw that's in pain?'

'I'm not sure,' Beth told him. 'It seems to be everywhere. She said it felt like red-hot pokers in her mouth.'

'All right, well, I won't dock her wages so long as you complete the march for her,' he said.

'I will,' Beth promised, although her feet were already sore from the short walk to Bow Station.

A moment later Harry blew his whistle. 'Let's go!'

The marchers linked arms and chanted over and over,

'And will the match trade die?

And will the match trade die?

Then thirty thousand working girls

Will know the reason why.'

Beth joined in with the chant as she was swept along with the marching crowd. But she couldn't stop thinking about poor Iris back at home.

They'd only gone half a mile when someone shouted, 'Peelers!'

Ahead of them were hundreds of police in their uniform of blue tailcoats and heavy boots. They held wooden truncheons as well as rattles and whistles.

Beth was terrified. Everyone knew peelers carried handcuffs and no one wanted to go to jail! She gave a cry as a policeman headed towards her, his truncheon raised. She put her hands over her head to protect herself, but he ran past her towards Harry, who was further back in the crowd.

'This is a peaceful march!' Harry shouted, but the policeman still struck him with his truncheon, tore the petition from his hands and stamped on it.

The police jostled and shoved and jeered at the marchers. Small children were screaming and crying. It was chaos.

'Keep going!' Harry shouted to Beth and the other protestors. 'Don't stop!'

And they'd pressed on, marching through the madness with quick strides.

Luckily more and more match-worker tax protestors joined the march as they headed into central London and the police fell back at the sheer numbers. The chanting began again and grew stronger. *'And will the match trade die? And will the match trade die?'*

They passed a stall selling boiled sheep's trotters. Beth didn't like the smell at all, but it still made her stomach rumble. When they passed stalls selling delicious hot roasted nuts she almost drooled.

And here they were now, standing in front of the huge Houses of Parliament, where there had been still more protestors waiting to join them.

She looked behind her at the crowd – the marchers stretched further than Beth could see.

'Must be thousands of protestors, maybe even tens of thousands!' Harry told Beth. He rubbed his arm where the police truncheon had struck him. 'Mister Gladstone will *have* to listen to us now.'

Beth nodded with a funny giddy feeling in her hungry belly. She could hardly believe it. Poor people like them telling the prime minister he was wrong!

Chapter 2

Scamp was bored. He'd shredded the whole of the newspaper page and was still the only cat that was wide awake. He pounced on a ball of knitting wool that had rolled on to the floor.

'No, Scamp!' the maid hissed, scooping up the wool and shooing him away.

Scamp jumped up on to his favourite spot on the windowsill instead and then clawed his way up the heavy curtains. His ears twitched at the *clack clack* of the maid's needles as she resumed her knitting. He peered down from his new perch on the curtain rail to watch. His eyes followed the tiny flashes of the needles as they caught the late-afternoon sunlight.

'There now, Mister Bismarck, aren't you a beauty?' another maid told a big white cat who was sitting purring on her lap.

Scamp's head tilted. He listened to the whistling breath of the elderly lady, who had fallen asleep at her writing desk with a letter resting on her lap.

The window had been left open a few inches at the very top to let in some fresh air. A sudden gust came through and ruffled Scamp's long fur. He turned to look out of the window and stared at a tree just outside. Its branches were full of white blossom that brushed against the glass. Birds flew in and out with twigs in their beaks, busily building their nests.

Scamp left the curtain rail for the narrow window frame. There was just enough space for a small kitten to push his head through the gap and then squeeze his body through after. A moment later he'd leapt from the frame on to an outstretched tree branch.

He darted a glance back at the window and saw the door open and young George walk into the cats' room, followed by his mother. George had bowls of rice pudding on a tray. Scamp liked rice pudding very much. He *miaow*ed but no one inside the room heard him or even looked over at the window. Even if they had, he was half hidden by white blossom.

'Oh, is it rice pudding time already?' the old lady asked, waking up at the sound of the door.

'Yes, Miss Nightingale,' said George.

Scamp watched as George and his mother laid sheets of newspaper on the carpet and set the cats' food bowls down. He'd never been outside the house before and had no idea how to get back in. He *miaow*ed again, louder this time, as the cats started to lap at their five o'clock treat.

Scamp was still watching them eating when a carrion crow flew on to his branch and made him jump. He cowered as the huge black bird hopped towards him, its eyes sharp and its beak menacing. Scamp froze in fear, but a second later the bird raised its wings, the tips like long fingers, and he bolted into action, half running, half falling down the tree and away.

The pavement was hard and cold beneath his tender paws as he raced along the street.

Suddenly he heard a loud, rasping *CAW!* as the crow dive-bombed him.

Scamp was so frightened he ran straight into the busy main road at the end of the street. He curled up in a quivering ball in the middle of the road as a stampede of horses' hooves thundered towards him. The driver of the mail coach didn't see the kitten, but luckily the four horses did and side-stepped him. As soon as they'd gone Scamp jumped up, ran to the other side of the road, through a pair of metal gates and into a vast area of greenery, his little heart beating very quickly.

'Close the curtains, George,' Miss Nightingale said.

'Yes, Miss Nightingale.'

'And stir up the fire; it's getting chilly in here now the sun's gone.'

George prodded at the fire with a poker and the small flames flickered and grew.

It wasn't long before all of the rice pudding bowls were licked clean, and he collected them up and took them back to the kitchen. It was only as he was helping his mother to wash and dry them that he realized he hadn't seen one of the cats. His eyebrows creased in concern. Scamp, the little calico kitten with the black patch of fur over one eye, *loved* rice pudding. He was usually the first to jump at the 5 o'clock treat.

Maybe he ate it really quickly before I saw him, George thought as he dried the last of the bowls and put it away. *He's probably back in his hiding place under the sofa right now.*

Miss Nightingale had so many cats that sometimes it was just about impossible to keep an eye on all of them. Especially one as cheeky as Scamp. George grinned as he thought about how Scamp's big innocent eyes belied the fact he was always getting himself into trouble.

He thought he'd better go back to the cats' room, just to check on the little kitten.

*

'Scamp?' George said, kneeling down and looking under the sofa. 'Scamp?' He wriggled his fingers and tapped them on the carpet, expecting the kitten to jump out and pounce. But not today.

'Where are you, Scamp?' George said, an edge of panic in his voice now.

He spotted a paw poking out from under one of the armchairs, but when he looked more closely he found it was only Soyer.

'It's just me, Soyer,' George said as the scaredy-cat backed away even further.

When he looked under the bureau, Tom and Topsy thought he wanted to play and jumped on to his back with excited chirrups. But George was getting more concerned by the minute.

'Could dear little Scamp have slipped out when the door was opened to bring in the rice pudding?' Miss Nightingale said, looking up from the letter she was reading.

'I'll check,' George said, his stomach churning.

Soon most of the staff of number 10 South Street were searching the house from top to bottom. But Scamp was nowhere to be found.

'Oh, I do hope he hasn't got *outside* somehow,' Miss Nightingale said when George relayed the bad news with a knot in his stomach. 'The traffic in Park Lane can be horrendous and the wheels of the coaches are so noisy they make my head hurt. The mail coach is the worst of all – it stops for no one in its haste to deliver the post on time!'

'I'll find him,' George said, his voice sounding stronger than he felt. 'He can't have gone far.'

George headed out of the house with Albert the footman and Edward, Miss Nightingale's elderly horse carriage driver. On the steps they passed the delivery man who'd brought the late editions of the newspapers.

'Have you seen a calico kitten?' George asked him hopefully.

'Cali-what now?' the delivery man said.

'Calico,' George repeated. 'It means his fur is black, white and ginger.'

'Nope,' the man said. Then his eyes grew wide. 'Is he one of Miss Nightingale's cats? I'll come and help you look for him. Everyone knows how important Miss Nightingale's cats are to her.'

George nodded eagerly. They had to find Scamp as soon as possible and he was glad of the help.

The cool green grass was much softer on Scamp's tender paws than the hard road had been and his heartbeat gradually slowed back to normal. The crow had gone and the kitten watched as a sparrow pecked at a worm and then flew off with it in its beak. A squirrel ran across the grass just ahead and, feeling much better, Scamp gave chase until it ran up a tree. He stared at the squirrel, willing it to come down. But it just looked at him loftily, safe in the branches.

There was a yap to the side of him and Scamp turned to see a brown-and-white puppy running across the grass towards him, tail wagging. Scamp had never met a dog before and he hastily darted away, past a fountain of a boy and dolphin in a sunken rose garden and on into the woods of the Dell.

At last he curled up among the bluebells and closed his eyes, only to hear a growl a few seconds later. His eyes flew open to see a fox looming over him with its sharp white teeth bared. Scamp jumped up and ran for his life with the fox right behind him. The sound of its ragged breaths filled his ears as it got closer and closer.

He raced along the wooden boards of a fishing jetty. He didn't see the lake until it was too late – and he fell in with a *splash*. Instinctively, he paddled his paws back and forth, trying to keep his head above the water. Ducks swam over to him, quacking, as Scamp paddled round and round in a small circle. The fox stood on the edge of the jetty looking down at the ducks and drooling.

'Night, then, Joe,' a voice said.

Scamp tried to *miaow* for help, but ended up with a mouthful of water instead. The fox slunk away into the bushes.

'See you in the morning, Ted.'

'Hope we catch more fish tomorrow,' a third man said. 'Hardly worth coming here today. And I thought the Serpentine was supposed to be plentiful!'

'Might as well leave the landing nets here – they're all empty,' said the last man.

None of them noticed a small kitten thrashing about in the lake and desperately trying to get out.

As the fishermen headed for home Scamp finally stopped circling and paddled to the edge of the lake, his head bobbing under the water as he struggled to stay afloat.

The lake had been easy for the kitten to fall into, but it was impossible to get out of in the same way. Scamp's tired legs swam over to the reed bed next to the jetty. He didn't even see the swans' nest hidden among the reeds that towered over him until it was nearly too late.

One of the territorial swans stretched out its long neck towards him and the other one flapped its enormous wings. Scamp gave a cry of fear and promptly fell into a large rope landing net at the edge of the Serpentine, half in the mud and half in murky water. His paws clung desperately to the netting as he watched the swans circling him, just out of reach.

Chapter 3

Beth stared up at the magnificent Palace of Westminster, bathed in a golden glow from the setting sun. She wished she could draw a picture of it to show Iris. It was like a magical fairy-tale castle and as different from where she and her sister lived as could be. How could the men who worked inside it possibly understand what it was like not to have clean water or enough food to eat, to live in a single damp room with people in the next one so close you could hear them turn over in bed?

Beth wasn't sure the Members of Parliament who worked in Westminster could *ever* understand why the extra penny tax would be so devastating for the match-workers. But she knew they had to try.

'And will the match trade die?
And will the match trade die?
Then thirty thousand working girls
Will know the reason why.'

Along with the rest of the protestors Beth shouted the chant over and over at the closed latticed windows. But no one came out to speak to them.

'Just ignoring us,' a gaunt woman said, holding her baby close.

'They must have heard us, though,' Harry told her. 'The whole of London must have heard!'

The woman nodded, but she didn't look too sure. 'Poor's invisible to rich folks,' she muttered as she kissed her baby's tear-strewn cheek.

Gradually, the protestors gave up waiting for someone to come out of the palace and started the long walk home.

'Work tomorrow – any chance we can come in late, Harry?'

Harry shook his head. 'Six thirty, as usual.'

Beth stared at the wonderful sunset over the Houses of Parliament. She longed to paint it and hold its beauty in her heart forever. She sighed. She didn't even *own* any paints. Still, she wished Iris was there to see the sunset too.

'Looks like it's going to rain in a bit.'

'Better be getting back.'

'At least we tried.'

Finally, Beth tore her eyes away from the magnificent sky and gave up too. Only by now there was no one left whom she recognized and she had no idea of the way home.

The streets were crowded with people and traffic hurrying home. Beth headed down one street and then back up another, but nowhere looked familiar. She was realizing much too late that she hadn't paid attention to the route they'd taken on the way. Her feet were so sore and she was so hungry she was hardly able even to think. All she knew was that she was tired beyond tired and walking in circles.

Beth wrapped her mother's shawl round her to try to keep warm as she trudged along, until, eventually, she found herself in front of the wrought-iron gates leading to Hyde Park.

'Just a brief rest,' she told herself as she headed inside and sat down on a bench. She felt so exhausted, but knew she had to regain her strength. She thought of Iris, asleep in bed. She would be worried sick if she woke up and Beth wasn't home.

But no sooner had Beth sat down than she saw a policeman in the distance heading her way. With a jolt she remembered the terror of being cornered by the police during the march. She darted behind a rhododendron bush nearby and crouched down among the purple flowers. The policeman whistled as he walked past the bush, his truncheon swinging in one hand. Beth held her breath as she watched him through the leaves.

He'd almost gone past when a twig cracked under Beth's foot. She put her hand over her mouth to stop herself from making a sound, but the policeman didn't even turn his head towards her hiding place.

She breathed a sigh of relief as he continued on his way without blowing his whistle or raising his wooden truncheon.

Safe, Beth thought as she watched the policeman head through the exit gates. She sat back down on the bench and rested her back against it. It felt so comfortable; she closed her eyes and a moment later fell fast asleep.

It was twilight when a hand roughly shook her shoulder. She opened her bleary eyes and saw a boy peering down at her. She shrank away in fear and confusion.

'Have you seen a pedigree Persian kitten?' the boy demanded sharply.

'Seen what?' Beth asked, rubbing her eyes. She was still befuddled from sleep. The boy looked to be about her own age.

'Cal-i-co – Pers-ian – kit-ten,' he said, spacing the words out as if he thought she was stupid. 'Miss-ing.'

'What's a calico Persian kitten look like?' Beth asked.

'White, black and ginger. Big eyes, really fluffy,' the boy told her. 'If you do see it, it belongs to a lady who lives in South Street, just off Park Lane.' He nodded across the park to the gates Beth had walked in through. 'Number ten. She's offering a reward of five shillings.'

Beth's eyes widened. Five shillings was much more than Iris earnt in a whole week, and that was working twelve-hour days!

If she found the kitten, they'd have a whole week's wages without Iris having to work. They'd be able to eat their fill and maybe even get Beth some shoes that fitted.

'Well, have you seen it?' the boy said.

'No,' Beth admitted, so he hurried off.

For a moment, Beth watched him retreat, trying to clear her head. Then, as the thought of the five shillings cut through the last remnants of sleep, she jumped up. Why shouldn't *she* look for the kitten too?

Around her she could hear other people calling its name: 'Scamp! Scamp!'

Gradually, the voices dwindled as the searchers headed further afield.

Beth sipped some water from a fountain in the shape of a boy and a dolphin before heading down a path towards a large lake. Two swans were close to the edge of it by the reeds. Beth had never seen swans before and she thought how beautiful they were and how graceful they looked.

The swans glided away as Beth approached.

As she watched them she heard the faintest of sounds, a plaintive mewling. The sound of a kitten! Beth's heart quickened. Could it be the lost kitten? She followed the sound to the edge of the lake where a little wooden fishing platform jutted out into the water. At the side of the platform, in a very muddy spot among the reeds, was a large fishing net and it was from this that the mewling sound was coming. Beth knelt down and gently pulled the net towards her. The mewling grew louder and now she saw that inside the net was a bedraggled, soaking wet, terribly thin kitten. It had got itself tightly tangled in the net and looked very distressed.

'It's all right. There now. You're safe,' Beth said, trying to untangle the net. Only it was heavy and awkward, and as she struggled to free the kitten she splattered it with even more mud. She did her best to dry the shivering creature with her mother's shawl. 'I'm sorry I don't have any food for you,' she said. She was feeling dizzy with hunger herself and wondered if the kitten had jumped into the net after a tasty fish. She smiled at the thought. 'I hope you're not as hungry as I am.' She cradled the soggy kitten and stroked its head. 'Poor little thing, all alone out here. Could you be the missing kitten?'

She remembered that the boy had mentioned a fluffy Persian cat. *This* kitten was so scrawny she was sure it couldn't have eaten in days. It couldn't be the same one the boy was talking about. It was still shivering and shaking, and she could feel its little ribs and its heart fluttering.

'Scamp?' she said. 'Is your name Scamp?'

The kitten didn't look up at her, just continued to shake in her hand. She thought of that other missing kitten, the one called Scamp, hopefully plump and cosy and warm beneath a bush or a tree. They'd probably found that one by now. What a coincidence that she should find a little kitten too.

'Are you hungry?' asked Beth, and now it finally looked up at her with its beautiful amber eyes. She thought about what to do. Surely she couldn't just leave this tiny creature to fend for itself. She looked out across the darkening park. At number 10 South Street there lived a lady who loved her own missing cat enough to offer a giant reward for its safe return. Perhaps that lady would be kind enough to give this poor little stray a few scraps. Beth's own tummy rumbled at the thought, but she supposed the kitten needed food more than her. It looked so desperately thin.

'We'll ask the lady if she can spare a morsel of food for you,' she told the kitten as she carried it across the lawn, out of the park, across the road and up the steps to number 10 South Street.

Chapter 4

The kitten wriggled inside Beth's arms as she pulled the bell rope.

'It's all right, don't be frightened,' she said.

The kitten tucked its head back inside her shawl.

The boy she'd seen in the park opened the door. He looked worried and tired.

'Have you found it?' he asked her, his voice sounding hopeful and desperate at the same time.

'No, but this poor little kitten could do with some food,' Beth said. 'I found him trapped in a net close to the lake.'

'Miss Nightingale can't be expected to feed every waif and stray . . .' the boy began, but then he trailed off. He was frowning as he stared at the kitten poking its head out of Beth's shawl.

'Miss Nightingale?' Beth said, hardly able to believe it. 'Do you mean Miss Florence Nightingale?'

The boy nodded and Beth gasped. *Florence Nightingale!* The nurse who'd helped the soldiers in the Crimean War. *Everyone* had heard of her. The lady with the lamp was probably the most famous woman in England apart from the Queen.

The kitten pushed its muddy head further out of the shawl and looked up at the boy with its big eyes.

41

'That's him!' the boy shouted excitedly.

'What is?' Beth asked absently. She'd been craning her neck to look inside the grand house, hoping she might catch a glimpse of the great lady.

'The missing kitten, of course! Did you find him? Or –' his eyes narrowed – 'did you steal him in the first place?' Now he looked suspicious as if he thought Beth was a thief.

'No, no, I didn't steal it – I wouldn't!' Beth said, outraged. 'I wouldn't steal anything from Miss Nightingale. She's a hero.'

But the boy wasn't listening. He was eagerly lifting the kitten out of Beth's shawl.

'Miss Nightingale will be so pleased when she sees you!' he said.

Before Beth could say another word he'd closed the heavy black wooden door in her face.

Her mouth fell open in surprise. What about the reward? Or at least a thank-you! She rang the bell pull again, but no one answered. She tried once more, but still there was no reply. She sank down on to the steps of the grand town house in sudden despair. It was such a long walk home and she didn't even know where she was going to find the energy to begin. It was all she could do not to cry. But poor, sick Iris would be so worried when she didn't return.

She pulled the woollen shawl round her shoulders and wished for the millionth time that she still had her mam. She stood up and slowly headed back down the steps.

'Scamp's been found!' George shouted, bursting into the cats' room with the kitten in his arms. Scamp was so exhausted he could barely even lift his head.

'Oh, I am so pleased,' Miss Nightingale said as George passed Scamp over, still wet and muddy. 'And was it you who found him, George?'

George looked into Miss Nightingale's face and very much wanted to say it was. But her sharp eyes never missed a trick. He hesitated and she smiled gently.

'And so who do we have to thank for Scamp's safe return?' she asked him.

'A girl. I don't know her name,' George said, looking at the floor.

'And how did you show our gratitude?' Miss Nightingale enquired.

George looked down at his shoes. 'I didn't,' he muttered.

'I suppose you at least gave her the reward?'

After a moment George shook his head. He didn't have five shillings – he'd forgotten all about the reward. He'd been too excited about telling Miss Nightingale that Scamp had been found even to think of it.

'Quick! Quick now! Run after Scamp's rescuer before she's gone too far and bring her back here,' Miss Nightingale told him. 'I want to give her the reward and thank her properly.'

George nodded. Miss Nightingale was right. The girl did deserve a reward for finding little Scamp. He raced down the steps of number 10 as fast as his legs would go and out of the front door. He stopped to think for a moment. He'd met the girl sleeping in Hyde Park – perhaps she'd gone back there. It was almost completely dark now. The park was just ahead of him and suddenly he saw a small figure, skinny shoulders wrapped in the shawl Scamp had been huddled inside. She was about to walk through the gates.

'Wait! Wait!' he yelled. 'Hey, you! Kitten-finder!'

Beth stopped in surprise and turned to see the boy who'd shut the door in her face running down the street towards her.

'What do you want now?' she asked him rather more bitterly than she'd intended. But her feet were aching and she was so tired.

'Miss Nightingale wants to meet you,' the boy gasped when he reached her. 'Come on – she doesn't like to be kept waiting!'

'Miss Nightingale?' Beth said slowly. 'Miss Florence Nightingale wants to meet *me*?'

'Yes, yes, yes,' George said. 'Miss Nightingale, the most famous woman in England – apart from the Queen, of course – wants to meet you. Now will you hurry up?'

When Beth still didn't move quickly enough he grabbed her arm and half dragged her down the street to number 10.

'Miss Nightingale will want to know every detail, so don't leave anything out. She's as sharp as a knife and doesn't miss a thing,' he said as they went in.

As Beth followed the boy across the hallway, they passed a room on the ground floor containing shelves full of books from floor to ceiling. Beth didn't think she'd ever seen quite so many. She thought there must be more books in that one space than in the whole of her school!

Upstairs in the cats' room Scamp looked, wide-eyed, at the willow-patterned china bowl full of warm water and gave a *miaow* of protest. He did *not* want to get in. Soyer watched from a safe distance away underneath an armchair.

'Come on now, we can't have you all dirty, can we?' said Miss Nightingale and she nodded at the maid who was holding Scamp.

'That's it now, dearie,' the maid said as she lowered him into the warm water.

Scamp wriggled about and made little crying sounds.

'He looks so tiny and thin when he's all wet,' Miss Nightingale said. 'Almost impossibly so for a little kitten that loves to eat so much! Some cats like to swim or so I've been told. It doesn't appear that Scamp is one of them!'

Scamp certainly didn't like being washed, but when the maid lifted him out and dried him with a big fluffy towel he very much enjoyed that part of it and started to make happy little sounds instead.

'This way,' the boy said. Beth followed him up the stairs and into a kitchen where a lady was chopping fish. 'I'm George. That's my mother; she's one of the cooks,' he said.

'Hello, dear,' the lady smiled and Beth bobbed a curtsy. Her own mother had taught her how to do so when she was teaching her good manners.

'I'm Beth,' she told them.

George handed her a damp towel. 'Well, Beth, wipe your face and hands before you go in to see Miss Nightingale,' he said. 'She's most particular when it comes to cleanliness and germs.'

Beth rubbed her face and hands with the towel and did her best to smooth down her hair. Her heart was beating very quickly.

'Come on,' George said as soon as she was done. He gently knocked on the door of a room a little further down the corridor and when a high voice called, 'Come in!' he turned the handle and pushed the door open.

'This is the girl who found Scamp,' he told the elderly lady within.

Beth couldn't help but stare at all the cats and kittens in the room, lying on the furniture and velvet cushions on the floor. There were cats everywhere! A ginger, white and black kitten, wrapped in a towel, was sitting on the lap of a woman in a maid's uniform. It was making little mewling sounds as the maid stroked it.

The elderly lady was sitting at a writing desk. Her face lit up with a smile as she held out her hand to Beth.

'Hello, my dear,' she said, and Beth's face burned red because she knew she must look a right mess after walking all day in the wind and then rescuing the muddy kitten from the net. She was just glad Miss Florence Nightingale wasn't yet in the room to see her. She'd learnt all about the great lady at school in Ireland and in England; how she and her nurses had gone out to the war-torn Crimea and helped the wounded British soldiers. How every night Florence Nightingale had barely slept but had visited the injured soldiers instead, carrying a lamp to light her way, and had whispered words of comfort to them. Beth's teacher, Miss Morrow, had showed them the picture of the tall, slim, dark-haired Miss Nightingale holding the lamp and tending the wounded soldiers that had been published in the *Illustrated London News*. Miss Morrow had carefully cut it out and kept it safe pressed between the leaves of a book. She'd also shown the children a photograph of Miss Nightingale looking straight into the camera with her hands clasped in front of her. The photograph had been printed on a postcard and was much less fragile than the newspaper clipping. Miss Morrow had told the children she'd bought it from a news stand.

Beth wondered if the elderly lady could be Miss Nightingale's mother. She did think she noticed something familiar round the eyes.

George nudged Beth when she didn't respond to the greeting.

'It-it's an honour to meet you, madam,' she stammered.

'And I to meet you. What is your name, dear?'

'Beth,' Beth told her. 'My full name's Elizabeth, but everyone calls me Beth.'

'Well, Beth, I am most grateful to you for finding Scamp and returning the little imp to us. Please accept this as a small token of our gratitude.' The old lady nodded to George and he took a small velvet bag from the writing desk and handed it to Beth. The coins inside the bag clinked.

'Th-thank you,' Beth stammered as she took the reward and put it safely in her pocket. Iris was going to be amazed when she returned home with five whole shillings.

At that moment the kitten that had been wrapped in a towel on the maid's lap jumped out of her arms and came running over.

It rubbed its face against her ankles and Beth instinctively knelt down to stroke it.

'Oh! It's you!' she said in surprise when the kitten looked up. 'Well, don't you look different? Who'd have thought under all that mud you'd be a beautiful ginger, black and white!'

'Calico,' George said.

'I know,' said Beth, remembering.

The kitten was barely recognizable as the bedraggled creature she'd rescued. But she knew it was him from his big amber eyes – she'd know them anywhere. She loved the little patch of black fur he had over one of his eyes, giving him a mischievous look.

'I'm so glad you're home safe and sound,' Beth told the kitten.

Scamp rubbed his head against her hands and purred.

'He should have come running over to me not you,' George said sulkily to Beth. 'I'm the one who spent hours searching for him!'

'Cats like who they like,' the elderly lady told George. 'I'm sure one day one of the cats will favour you.'

George looked disgruntled. 'Scamp liked me well enough before he met *her*,' he said almost under his breath.

Scamp pushed his little furry head under Beth's hand and purred as she stroked him.

'Perhaps you have a kitten or a cat of your own?' the elderly lady asked Beth.

Beth shook her head. She'd never even stroked a kitten before. There was a cat that stalked the alleyway near where she and her sister lived, but it wouldn't let anyone come near it. No one had pets in their neighbourhood, no one could afford to, although the alley cat got plenty of food from all the rats that lived there too.

'Well, Scamp certainly does seem to be taken with you,' the elderly lady said with a soft smile.

'And me with him,' said Beth. 'I thought he was just a poor lost little kitten no one wanted. He was covered in mud, soaked through and shivering from the cold. I cuddled him to me and did my best to dry him with my mother's shawl. But now I find that he actually lives in a palace!'

'Oh, this is hardly a palace,' the old lady said. 'Vicky has over seven hundred rooms at Buck House.'

Beth's mouth fell open as she realized the 'Vicky' being referred to was actually Queen Victoria.

She looked at the elderly lady from underneath her eyelashes, wondering just who she was. She did look a little like the famous photograph of Miss Nightingale her teacher had bought as a postcard from a news stand, but that Miss Nightingale was much, much younger.

'You look a little confused, my dear,' the elderly lady said.

Beth was confused, but she also felt shy and a bit embarrassed.

'It's just – it's just I thought I was going to meet Miss Florence Nightingale . . . and you don't look like the photograph of her,' she stammered. She could feel her face getting hot and knew it must be turning red.

'Ah! The photograph!' the elderly lady said with a wry smile. 'That photograph was taken by order of the queen when I returned from the Crimea back in eighteen fifty-eight. Probably before you were even born!'

Beth nodded.

'When I arrived at the palace, Her Majesty insisted it be done and so I sat for it. As it's about the only photograph there is of me in circulation, it's as if time stopped and I never grew a day older! But of course, like everyone else, I have. I do so hate having my photograph taken – I can't bear even to look at drawings or paintings of myself.'

'But you couldn't refuse the queen, could you, Miss Nightingale?' George said.

'No, I could not,' Florence Nightingale agreed, 'and Vicky was utterly charming. She told me I had no self-importance or humbug and it was no wonder the soldiers loved me so.'

'So you really are Miss Florence Nightingale?' Beth said slowly to make sure.

'I am indeed, although an older version than the Nightingale in the photograph you've seen. People still insist on buying the thing, even though it's thirteen years old. When I returned from the Crimea, the almost fatal illness I suffered there left me barely recognizable as the woman I'd been. I had to have all my hair cut off too to reduce the fever.'

'But it grew back,' George said and Beth nodded. She could see Miss Nightingale had plenty of hair tucked under her cap.

Miss Nightingale sighed. 'I hate all the fuzz-buzz about me in the newspapers too. I think it would be a lot better if people got on with their own business instead of reading about other people's lives!

'But enough about me. It's very fortunate indeed for us that you brought Scamp here rather than taking him home with you,' she said. 'Especially when you thought he was just some poor lost stray.'

Beth smiled to herself as she shook her head. She would never have taken Scamp home with her. It wouldn't have been safe for him at all. He'd have been stolen if anyone saw him looking all brushed and clean like he did now and there would have been nothing at all for him to eat.

Thinking of home made Beth think of Iris. She would be really worried now it was so late, but how pleased she would be with the reward money!

Miss Nightingale was still talking, her bright eyes twinkling. 'Now, Beth, I want to hear all the details of how you rescued Scamp. May I ask, dear, what you were doing all by yourself in Hyde Park at this hour?'

'I was part of the match-girl march,' Beth told her. She looked out of the window. She didn't know how she was going to find her way home in the dark when she'd been lost in broad daylight. She bit her bottom lip.

'Ah, I read about the march in the late edition of the newspaper. And you, my dear, are you one of the match-workers?' Miss Nightingale asked her. 'You don't look old enough, but I know sometimes looks can be deceptive . . .'

Beth shook her head, but it did give her the horrible thought that one day soon she might be a match girl too. In only a few years' time she could be going to work at the Bryant and May factory day after day, just like her sister did. And suddenly she knew without a shadow of a doubt that she didn't want to do that. But would she have a choice? Iris certainly hadn't had one. It was the only way to make enough money to keep the pair of them out of the workhouse.

'No – I don't work there. Not yet. My older sister does, though, and we were going to march together. Only she came down with a terrible pain in her face this morning.'

Miss Nightingale's grey-blue eyes looked at her sharply.

'And what did her face look like?' she asked.

'Red,' Beth said, 'and her cheeks were swollen.'

'Could it be mumps?' Miss Nightingale asked.

Beth shook her head. 'We've both had mumps before and her pain wasn't like that.'

Miss Nightingale frowned. 'And your sister, did she say where the pain was coming from exactly?'

'She said her gums felt like they were being stabbed with red-hot pokers,' Beth told her.

It was strange how Harry, the foreman at the factory, had asked almost the same question.

'Let's hope she's feeling better when you return,' Miss Nightingale said, and then she turned her attention to Scamp. 'I expect you're hungry,' she remarked. 'He missed his rice pudding today – he always has a little at five o'clock, as do all my cats.'

Beth thought that rice pudding sounded wonderful, although she'd never tasted any. She was so hungry her head felt all swirly and she was so tired she could barely stand.

The room was very warm compared to the chill of outside.

'Never mind that now, little Scamp, there's fish for your supper and I'm sure it will suffice. Will you bring the cats' food in, George? And you, my dear, you must be hungry too,' Miss Nightingale said to Beth. 'Ask your mother to make some food for Beth, George.'

'Yes, Miss Nightingale,' George said, and he left the room.

But Beth didn't get to eat the food George brought in. Her head started to swim and the next moment she was having a lovely dream in which she sat down to a delicious feast. She didn't even know that she'd slipped to the floor.

'Beth! Beth, my dear, wake up,' Miss Nightingale called to her, but her voice seemed to be coming from far, far away and Beth's eyes remained closed.

Chapter 5

When Beth opened her eyes she immediately knew she wasn't in her own bed. Her second thought was of Iris, who certainly wasn't there. Beth was covered by a blanket and her head rested on a soft pillow. She sat up and found she was on one of the sofas, close to the window, in the room where she'd met Miss Florence Nightingale the night before. The room with all the cats in it. And the cats were still there – white ones and black ones, gingers and tabbies, big and small, young and old.

Scamp was curled up next to her and he rolled over on his back and stretched out his paws. Beth's first thought was of Iris and how worried she would be to wake up to find her little sister missing, but she couldn't resist giving the kitten a stroke.

'Good morning, Scamp,' Beth said softly.

He jumped up on to the back of the sofa and then on to the windowsill. He poked his head through the closed curtains, looked out at the white-blossomed tree and gave a *miaow*.

Beth knelt on the sofa and pulled back a corner of a curtain to look out of the window too. There were birds fluttering in and out of the tree, people on the pavement walking past, horses pulling carriages and carts, and beyond all of them was the great greenness of Hyde Park. Beth bit her bottom lip. She had to get home to Iris, but she couldn't just leave without saying thank you to Miss Nightingale.

'I expect you'd like to go out there, wouldn't you?' Beth said to Scamp. 'Even though the last time you did you landed yourself in lots of trouble!'

Scamp gave a *miaow* as if he were answering her and then looked back at the window.

Beth thought the little kitten looking wistfully out of the window would make a perfect picture. The waste-paper basket next to the bureau was almost full. She went over to it and took out a piece of paper without any writing on the back. There were pens and pencils in a metal holder and she took a pencil out, sat down at the writing desk and started to draw the kitten.

She wanted to get Scamp's ginger, white and black coat just right. But she only had a grey pencil to use so she made the black bits of his coat very dark, the ginger parts a lot lighter and the white patches she left unmarked.

Once Scamp was drawn she turned her attention to the tree outside, carefully sketching the blossoms on the branches and the birds that flew in and out of it.

She was so engrossed in her drawing she didn't notice the time ticking by.

'That is one of his favourite places to sit,' Miss Nightingale's sweet voice observed, making Beth jump and draw a jagged line through one of the blossoms she'd just drawn. Flustered, she stood and curtsied to the great lady who had come in behind her, accidentally knocking her drawing on the floor as she did so.

'Sometimes he spends the whole day just looking out of the window,' Miss Nightingale continued with a smile.

The cats in the room, who'd paid no attention to Beth, immediately rushed over to Miss Nightingale.

'Yes, yes, good morning to you and good morning to you,' she said as she greeted them. 'I hope you slept well, Mister Bismarck,' she said to a large white cat, 'and that you didn't get too close to the fireguard, Aggy!

'How are you feeling, my dear?' Miss Nightingale asked Beth, leaning heavily on George's arm as she came further into the room with the cats milling around her, purring. 'You gave us quite a fright. But what could have caused you to faint? When did you last eat?'

'Monday evening,' Beth said softly.

'Oh, my dear,' Miss Nightingale said, shaking her head. 'That will explain it. The body needs regular nourishment and good food to flourish.'

'She probably wants to be going home now,' George said.

Beth threw him a sharp look. She *did* want to go home very much to see how Iris was, but George sounded like he just wanted her to leave as soon as possible. She remembered how he had closed the front door in her face, and decided that she didn't like him very much.

George pulled the chair out from Miss Nightingale's desk and Miss Nightingale sat down.

'Thank you. Now go and get some food from the kitchen for Beth, George. And then you'd better be off to school – you don't want to be late.'

George sighed as he left the room.

'Sit down, Beth,' Miss Nightingale said. 'We don't want you fainting again. You'll feel much better once you've had something to eat.'

Beth sat down on the sofa she'd slept on and Scamp came to join her.

A few moments later, George came back with three slices of white bread on a blue-and-white patterned plate, together with a small jar of strawberry jam, a pat of yellow butter, a teapot in the same blue-and-white pattern, a jug of milk, a little bowl full of white cubes and a set of silver tongs. There was also a blue-and-white patterned cup and saucer and a small knife on the tray.

'Put it on the little table next to Beth,' Miss Nightingale told him.

George plonked the tray down with a rattle.

'Now, my dear, I want to see you eat a lot,' Miss Nightingale said to Beth.

'You've been so kind already,' Beth said. 'I don't know how to thank you.'

Miss Nightingale waved her hand. 'No need for that. Have you put a napkin on the tray, George?'

'No, Miss Nightingale.'

'Well, go and fetch one quickly now,' the lady replied.

'Yes, Miss Nightingale,' George said half-heartedly, and he left the room with a frown.

Beth poured some milk from the jug into the cup. She'd have liked to gulp it down and then gobble up all the food as fast as she could because she was so hungry and thirsty, but she managed not to. Her mother had taught her the importance of good manners. She'd wait for George to bring the napkin.

All of the crockery had the same blue-and-white design on it and Beth thought it was very beautiful. There were two birds in flight at the top, stylized pagodas dotted around as well as trees and a bridge across a stream with three men running over it.

Beth popped one of the white cubes into her mouth and smiled as it melted on her tongue. She'd never had a sugar cube before, but sometimes the family had eaten sugar biscuits at Christmas as a special treat.

George came back with both the morning newspaper and a napkin. He gave the news-paper to Miss Nightingale and the napkin to Beth.

'Thank you. Now off to school,' Miss Nightingale told him. 'George doesn't enjoy his lessons very much,' she told Beth when he reluctantly left the room. 'Do you go to school, my dear?'

'Yes – to the ragged school,' Beth told her. 'Lots of children go there, mostly orphans from the East End. When we lived in Ireland I went to a school in the village run by the nuns. Iris was an assistant teacher there and helped us with our reading and writing. Everyday we would learn something new.' She was sure George didn't go to a ragged school. He'd go to a proper one where they had plenty of paper and pencils for drawing.

Miss Nightingale opened the newspaper and began reading.

Beth dropped three cubes of sugar in the tea and sipped; it was so delicious she added a few more.

Miss Nightingale carried on reading the newspaper while Beth ate. But suddenly the lady exclaimed, 'Whose drawing is this?' She was holding the piece of paper that showed Beth's sketch of Scamp. She must have picked it up off the floor.

'I'm sorry,' Beth said around a mouthful of bread and jam. 'I didn't ... I thought the paper was ... was in the waste basket.' She swallowed painfully. The truth was she hadn't thought about what she was doing at all. The chance to draw Scamp was too much to resist. 'At school we don't have paper for drawing...'

They drew with chalk on a small easel when they were allowed to, which wasn't often.

When her family had first come to England, Beth had been to a proper school and liked nothing more than to draw, and her parents had encouraged her to do so. One of those drawings was now covering the broken window back at home.

Home. *Iris.* The bread felt lumpy in her empty stomach. Iris must be thinking something dreadful had happened to her by now.

'It's really a very good likeness of Scamp,' Miss Nightingale said, and Beth's face turned warm. She wouldn't be surprised if it looked as red as a beetroot. Miss Morrow had said she was very talented, but she'd never have thought that one day Miss Florence Nightingale would think so too!

Iris had joked that if they ended up truly destitute maybe Beth could chalk on pavements like they sometimes saw beggars doing. Only Beth was really frightened she'd be in trouble with the police if they caught her. She'd been frightened of the police before yesterday, but after the march she felt even more so.

Scamp jumped down from the windowsill and up on to the sofa next to Beth. She stroked his furry head.

'I love drawing him,' she said.

Miss Nightingale nodded. 'But who taught you to draw?'

'My da,' Beth smiled.

'And is he a talented artist too?' Miss Nightingale asked.

Beth nodded her head, remembering her father teaching Iris how to add depth to her drawings using perspectives. He'd used the small row of cottages they lived in with the village school in the middle, where Beth was a pupil and Iris was an assistant teacher, to show her.

'*See how the furthest one looks smaller — you draw it like this* . . .' Seven-year-old Beth had listened intently and learnt too. '*See where the sea and the sky meet, Beth, that's the horizon line,*' he'd told her. She swallowed hard and looked at Miss Nightingale who had her head tilted to one side, waiting for her reply. 'He was, but not any more,' she said. 'He and my mother passed away during the cholera epidemic three years ago.' A tear slipped down Beth's face. She missed them both so much. 'We hadn't long arrived from Ireland. My mother and father worked at the Bryant and May match factory where Iris works now.'

Sometimes late at night when the two of them were huddled up together in bed, Iris would talk about the time when they used to live in Ireland, where the rolling hills had led down to the beach.

'We were happy then. There was always enough to eat – not like now,' Iris would whisper to her.

Beth tried to remember the rolling hills for herself, but she couldn't truly picture them any more and thought she was probably just imagining them from her sister's stories. But she could just about remember the smell of the sea and the feel of the waves tickling her toes – and the sound of her father laughing as he scooped her up.

'There's a job waiting for me over in London,' her father had told the family. He'd made it sound like the most exciting thing in the world. To hear him you'd have thought the streets would be paved with gold and none of them would be hungry again. 'Your uncle's working at the Bryant and May match factory and they need more hands there. There's a terrible demand for matches in London.'

So they'd left Ireland and crossed the sea on a ferry. But the London streets were not paved with gold.

'Twenty-seven million matches a year the factory makes,' Beth's father told her as he swigged his tea after another long day at work. 'And what do the workers see from the profits? Barely a crumb.'

Beth's mam, da and sister had all been employed at the factory when the cholera struck. Iris hadn't caught it, but their mother and father had.

Beth swallowed hard to stop herself from crying in earnest. Life was so hard without them.

'Ah yes, the cholera caused a catastrophic epidemic in the East End,' Miss Nightingale said gently. 'It was a terrible, terrible time. They say three thousand people died, though it could have been more. When it comes to accurate recording, the poor are usually the ones most gravely underestimated.'

'A kind man named Doctor Barnardo came to see us,' Beth told her. 'He visited lots of the families and tried to help them. But there was nothing he could do to save my mam and da.'

'I'm so sorry to hear that,' Miss Nightingale said and she sounded like she truly was. 'I'm sure your parents were very fine people and I'd have liked to meet them.'

Beth nodded as she mopped her tears with the napkin. 'They would have been so honoured to have met you, Miss Nightingale.'

'Oh, pish-posh! I'm no one special,' Miss Nightingale said with a smile, but they both knew that wasn't true.

Beth watched as Scamp hopped off the sofa and stalked over to a small black-and-white cat for a play-wrestle.

'That's Aggy,' Miss Nightingale told her. 'The two of them love to play together. I sometimes like to name my cats and kittens after people I've met or heard of, and Aggy's named after an Irish nurse called Agnes Jones.'

'Have you been to Ireland?' Beth asked Miss Nightingale.

The lady nodded. 'A long time ago when I was a young woman, almost twenty years ago now! I wanted to visit a hospital in Dublin called St Vincent's, but it was closed when we got there. It was during the potato famine and I saw many desperate people.'

Beth nodded gravely. She knew all about that.

'I urged more help for the people of Ireland then as I do now for the millions of people facing starvation in India. I know if the government would only turn their full attention to the problem they could solve the Indian crisis just as they could have solved the one in Ireland. But their hearts must have turned to stone because as far as I can see nothing's being done to help at all.'

'Did you go to the hospital to learn how to be a nurse?' Beth asked, but Miss Nightingale shook her head.

'No, I learnt that from my time at the Kaiserworth Hospital in Germany. They treated me just like every other nurse there. It was the first time I didn't have a maid to do my hair for me and the first time I ever scrubbed a floor –'

'You scrubbed floors!' Beth said. It seemed impossible that a great lady like Miss Florence Nightingale could have done such a thing.

'Oh yes,' Miss Nightingale told her. 'And I learnt how important cleanliness is, as well as fresh air and good food, for a patient to recover from whatever ails them. *"Maintain the air within the room as fresh as the air without"* was what we were taught.'

Beth couldn't wait to get home and tell Iris all about her adventures and the reward she'd been given for rescuing Scamp. She could almost see Iris's happy face when she gave her the money. Now they'd be able to have more than enough to eat, at least for a while.

She looked up at the clock as the big hand reached nine and bit her lip. 'My sister will be so worried about me,' she said.

'Yes, you must return to her,' Miss Nightingale said. 'May I keep this drawing? It will help if Scamp gets lost again – he's such an adventurous little imp!'

But at that moment Scamp looked the picture of innocence curled up next to Aggy.

'Of course,' Beth said. It was Miss Nightingale's pencil she'd used and her paper she'd drawn the picture on after all.

Miss Nightingale pulled a coin from her purse. 'I wouldn't dream of not paying for such a fine picture,' she said.

'Oh no, you've already been so kind!' Beth said. 'It could be a gift, if you like.'

But Miss Nightingale insisted. 'I hope you will accept it,' she said. 'Because then I would feel happy commissioning you to draw sketches of all of my cats.'

Beth's eyes widened. 'You want me to draw all of them?' she gasped. Miss Nightingale had so many cats.

'You will be doing me a great favour if you agree,' Miss Nightingale said. 'If your drawings of the other cats are as accurate as this one, then I will be able to use them on Lost Cat posters, should any of my other pets go missing.'

'Oh – oh, in that case, I'd love to draw all of your cats,' Beth said.

'Good. Now, I'm sure you're eager to get home to your poorly sister, my dear, although sweet Scamp will miss you dreadfully when you go. Can you come back very soon?'

Beth nodded, a huge smile on her face. 'Yes, Miss Nightingale,' she said.

'Then I look forward to seeing you again,' the lady told her. 'Why don't you take the rest of the bread and jam for your sister? You can return the plate when you come back. Edward the coachman will take you home and bring you back here on Saturday morning at nine o'clock sharp. If that suits you?'

'It suits me very well,' Beth said.

She gave Scamp and Aggy a goodbye stroke and Scamp jumped up and tried to follow her out of the room when she opened the door.

'Oh no, I'm sorry, but you can't come too,' Beth told him. 'I'll see you very soon, though.' She gave him a quick scratch on the head.

As Edward helped her up the step into the horse-drawn carriage, Beth looked at the big upstairs window and saw Scamp looking out. His little front right paw was lifted and pressed to the glass. She could almost hear him *miaow*.

'I'll be back soon,' Beth said, although she knew he couldn't hear her.

Chapter 6

Beth had never travelled in a carriage before and as the horse clip-clopped into the East End she saw children running after them.

'Hey, mister!' children called out to Edward the coachman. 'Give us some money.'

'Spare a copper.'

'Whoa there,' Edward said to the horse, pulling on the reins, when they reached Beth's street.

'Oh, I've been so worried!' Iris cried, running out of the house as soon as she spotted

Beth through the window. She had a rag wrapped round her face. Edward opened the carriage door and helped Beth down with the plate of bread and jam.

Iris scooped Beth to her and hugged her so tightly Beth could barely breathe. 'I heard the police were at the march . . . I didn't know what could have happened to you!'

'I'll be back on Saturday at eight fifteen precisely to collect you,' the white-haired carriage driver told Beth.

'Thank you, Edward,' Beth said, as the horse clip-clopped on its way.

'Edward?' Iris said, one of her eyebrows raised very high. The rag had slipped and Beth could see her face looked even more swollen than yesterday morning. 'And what are you doing in a coach like a grand lady, may I ask? Where are you going to on Saturday at precisely eight fifteen? What's going on,

85

Beth? I'd say you were in trouble if you weren't holding a plate of bread and jam!'

'No, not in trouble – in fact, the complete opposite,' Beth told her, squeezing her sister's hand. 'Nothing to worry about at all.' But she was worried about her sister's face. It looked very sore.

'How's your face feeling?' she asked Iris once they were inside their small, dark, dingy room that doubled as a bedroom and a kitchen. 'Have the red-hot pokers stopped poking your gums?'

Iris shook her head. 'If anything, it's worse. My ears are hurting too now. Harry came to check on me after the march yesterday. He told me to be sure not to come into work until all the swelling has gone down. I was really surprised when he told me that because they're such slave drivers there. But maybe he thinks it's contagious. Once one person comes down with something at the factory, everyone seems to get it.' Iris frowned. 'His voice did sound a bit strange, though – as if, perhaps, he knew something I didn't.'

'The police hit Harry with a truncheon and took the match-workers' petition from him,' Beth said, remembering how terrified she'd been. Then she noticed Iris was looking hungrily at the plate of food she was still holding.

'Oh! This is for you, but I don't know if you'll be able to eat it with your sore mouth,' Beth said, as she passed Iris the plate.

'Nothing's going to stop me eating this!' Iris said, taking a mouthful and making *mmm-mmm* sounds. 'Not even a million red-hot pokers dancing on my gums!'

While she was eating Beth told her all about what had happened.

'Oh, my goodness!' Iris shrieked when Beth showed her the money she'd earnt from finding and returning Scamp.

'And I got another penny this morning for drawing him and on Saturday I'm returning to Miss Nightingale's house to sketch all of her cats, and she's got lots – and she's going to pay me!' Beth finished in a rush.

On Saturday morning Edward arrived promptly at 8.15 to pick Beth up in the carriage and take her to South Street for nine o'clock.

Beth was already waiting outside for him, wearing the shoes she'd bought from the flea market. Not brand-new ones, but they fitted comfortably and were even a little too big so there was room for her feet to grow.

'Have you got Miss Nightingale's plate?' Edward asked her and Beth nodded. It was safely wrapped in her mother's shawl ready to be returned.

'Do you know where to go?' he asked when he dropped her off.

'I think so,' Beth told him.

As she walked up the stairs of number 10 South Street, Beth wasn't even sure if Scamp would remember her. She so hoped he would.

Once inside, she tapped gently on the door to the cats' room and George's voice called out, 'Come in!'

As soon as she opened the door Scamp hopped off the windowsill and came running over to her.

'Oh, hello,' Beth smiled as she knelt down to stroke the kitten. 'It's so lovely to see you again.' His fur was even fluffier than the last time she'd seen him.

'He's just been brushed,' said George, who was sitting on a rug in front of the fire with a big white cat in his lap. 'All Miss Nightingale's cats are brushed every morning.'

Two maids were also engaged in brushing cats. One of the maids had a black cat on her lap.

'This is Gladstone,' the maid told Beth as Gladstone purred. 'And I'm Rose.'

'My name's Hazel,' the other maid said, 'and this elderly gentleman cat is Dickens; he's named after the famous writer Mister Charles Dickens!'

Beth gazed at the elderly ginger cat the maid was holding. Dickens looked so relaxed he was half asleep as the brush wafted along his fur. Under the sofa Beth spotted a grey cat with bright blue eyes peeping out.

'That's Soyer,' Rose told her, 'and he runs away when it's brushing time. Such a nervous little thing. Although he does love it once he's actually being brushed!'

'Miss Nightingale's in her bedroom,' George told Beth. 'She's not feeling too well today, but she still wants to see you.' He put the brush down. 'Back soon, Mister Bismarck,' he told the white cat. 'This way,' he said to Beth.

Scamp trotted behind Beth as she followed George. Miss Nightingale's chamber was on the same floor as the cats' room, a few doors along. George tapped gently.

'Come in,' called the familiar voice.

Miss Nightingale was lying in her bed propped up by pillows. There was a shelf of books within easy reach and a little vase of roses on the bedside table. Two cats, kittens, really, were lying on the silk bedspread surrounded by newspapers and letters.

Beth watched as Scamp slipped past her and headed over to the large window where birds were pecking at crumbs that had been put out on the sill.

'Hello, my dear Beth,' Miss Nightingale said. 'How good to see you again.'

'And you too, Miss Nightingale,' Beth said. 'But I'm sorry you're not well.'

'Oh, pish-posh, my weakness comes and goes. On days like today, when it comes, it's far easier to stay in bed where I can get my work done quite happily, especially with Tom and Topsy here too.' She stroked the two kittens on the bed. 'Please ask your mother to prepare some food and a drink for Beth, George, and I'll have a cup of tea myself now.'

'Yes, Miss Nightingale,' George said and he left the room.

Scamp hopped up on to the windowsill to watch the birds on the other side of the glass. At first the birds flew away, but they soon came back. It was as if they knew he couldn't reach them because they'd seen him sitting there many times before.

Topsy and Tom started to play-wrestle on the bed.

'Scamp came running as soon as I arrived,' Beth said. 'I thought he might have forgotten me.'

'Oh no,' Miss Nightingale said. 'Cats are really very clever and they don't forget people who've been kind to them.'

Scamp put his paw on the glass of the window and the birds flew away. When they returned a few seconds later, he lay down to watch them.

'I expect you're pleased there's no longer going to be a match tax,' Miss Nightingale said to Beth with a smile. When Beth frowned in confusion she added, 'Queen Victoria herself wrote to protest against it. Look! Her letter's right here in the paper.' She handed Beth one of the newspapers lying on the bed and Beth read haltingly.

A letter from the queen
to the Chancellor of
the Exchequer.

Above all it seems *certain* that this tax will seriously affect the manufacture and sale of matches, which is said to be the sole means of support of a vast number of the very poorest people and little children, especially in London.

The queen trusts that the Government will reconsider this proposal and try to substitute some other tax which will not press upon the poor.

'The government has decided to increase income tax for everyone instead,' Miss Nightingale told Beth.

'So the monster match-workers' march worked!' Beth laughed with relief. 'Iris is going to be so pleased! And all the other match girls at Bryant and May, including the home-workers – having less money each week would have been hardest of all on them.'

It was like a stormy grey cloud had now been lifted.

'The tax really was a very poor idea of Gladstone's in the first place,' Miss Nightingale said. 'And your sister, Iris. Tell me about her. Has the pain in her face improved at all? I have a tincture that might help, if it is toothache rather than a pain in her jaw, but I don't want to give it to her until we can be sure where the pain is coming from and what is causing it. Giving a patient incorrect medicine could do more harm than good as well as delaying the proper treatment.'

'It hasn't gone, no,' Beth told Miss Nightingale. 'In fact, it's worse than it was. She's got earache too now and can barely sleep at night. Harry, the foreman from the factory, told her not to come into work until the swelling in her face has gone down completely.'

Miss Nightingale tilted her head to one side as she considered what to do for the best.

'Do you think you could draw your sister's face for me?' she said at last. 'The drawing must be accurate, mind you, Beth – as accurate as it can be. Ideally, I would see the patient, but I rarely venture out any more when I'm in London, and your sister shouldn't be forced to come here in her state. However, a careful, *detailed* drawing by you – one from each side of her face and another, or maybe two, from the front . . . and, in fact, one looking up from underneath her chin . . . well, yes, that should suffice.'

Beth nodded. She wasn't at all sure Iris would like having her face drawn, but she'd give it a go. Maybe she could draw her without Iris realizing what she was doing. It wouldn't be easy! And she'd need to buy some paper and a pencil.

'I thought you could use these,' Miss Nightingale said, almost as if she had read her mind. She was pointing to a set of pencils and some charcoal as well as two brand-new sketchbooks, one large and one small. Beth gasped with delight.

Her voice caught in her throat when she tried to speak. 'Th-thank you so much,' she said.

Miss Nightingale shook her head with a gentle smile. 'To get the best work one must have the best tools,' she said.

George tapped at the door and came in with a tray.

'Thank you, George,' Miss Nightingale said with a smile.

George looked over at the sketchbooks and pencils Miss Nightingale had given Beth. His lips pressed together and he frowned.

'Have all the cats been brushed, George?' the lady asked him.

'Almost all of them, Miss Nightingale; I was just finishing off Mister Bismarck. We haven't done Topsy and Tom because they slept in here last night. Rose managed to catch Soyer and give him a brush.'

'I'll see to Topsy and Tom myself,' Miss Nightingale said, 'and perhaps you, Beth, would like to give Scamp a brush?'

'I'd love to, Miss Nightingale,' Beth said.

'I've already done him,' George muttered.

'I'm sure he would love a second brush. That'll be all for now, George,' Miss Nightingale said. 'Why don't you go outside and play – maybe even go fishing. It's such a lovely day.'

'Which cat would you like me to draw first?' Beth asked Miss Nightingale when George had gone.

'Oh, dear little Scamp again, don't you think?' Miss Nightingale told her. 'He has been our most recent escapee. I just hope he hasn't got a taste for exploring now.'

'I think being trapped in the fisherman's net may have put him off exploring for a while!' Beth said.

Scamp was now curled up on the windowsill fast asleep. The two of them looked at him and laughed.

Beth opened the box of pencils and set to work in her new sketchbook while Miss Nightingale read through her morning's correspondence.

*

'I do so appreciate the care and detail you put into your work,' Miss Nightingale told Beth when she'd finished sketching Scamp and showed it to her. 'Precision is something I value most highly. The next time Scamp goes missing, if he does, we'll be able to use your picture for the posters. If having one's picture taken wasn't so unbearably slow I would get the cats' portraits taken, but you can't expect a cat to sit perfectly still for as long as a person can. Even for a human, three minutes sitting motionless can seem like a very long time indeed. They use head braces on people, you know, to stop them moving an inch! Maybe you should make a few more drawings of little Scamp now, one from the front and one from the side.'

'I expect he'd like to be outside too,' Beth said.

At that moment Scamp woke up and *miaow*ed at the window. Beth could see a squirrel finishing off the last of the birds' food.

Miss Nightingale nodded. 'I'm sure he would. But it isn't safe for a pedigree kitten to be wandering about all alone.'

And that gave Beth an idea. 'Maybe he could have a lead like a little dog – and then I could take him for a walk! Or George could,' she added as an afterthought.

'Well, now that might be a very good idea,' Miss Nightingale said. 'The ancient Egyptians used to have their cats on leads, you know. Although I think a harness would be better than a lead for a fragile kitten.'

Beth nodded. 'Something soft but strong.'

'Like a bandage!' Miss Nightingale said. Beth grinned – a bandage would be perfect.

Miss Nightingale took a bandage from her bedside table and when Beth had carried Scamp over to her she wrapped the two ends over the kitten's back and then round his tummy, looped them together, tied them so they wouldn't slip off and then handed them to Beth.

'Rather like making reins for a child,' Miss Nightingale said. 'Although much smaller, of course. Just a short walk for Scamp's first time, I think. And, of course, if he hates the harness, we'll think of something else for him.'

Scamp looked up at Beth, gave a *miaow* and jumped off the bed.

'Shall we go for a walk?' Beth asked him. She didn't know if the kitten had understood her, but he didn't try to pull away and the very tip of his tail flicked ever so slightly back and forth when they headed out of the room.

George was sitting on the floor outside.

'What are you doing there?' Beth asked him.

But George had a question of his own. 'Why's Scamp got a bandage wrapped round him?'

'It's his harness.'

'Looks like a half-wrapped Egyptian mummy!'

Beth couldn't help laughing. Miss Morrow had told them about mummies and showed them a picture of one, and of the great pyramids of Egypt. Beth longed to see them for herself some day.

Scamp had started stalking close to the wall – Beth thought he must have smelt something exciting. His front paws patted a gap in the wood, where George told her they suspected a mouse family were hidden. Beth and George watched and then followed him a little further down the corridor.

'Scamp really doesn't seem to mind his new harness at all,' Beth said when she and the little cat came back into Miss Nightingale's room a few minutes later. 'Although I think it is because he's such a curious kitten that he's too busy sniffing spots and prodding at places with his paws to notice he has a harness on at all. I let him go where he liked and I mostly just followed him. I'm pretty sure he started tracking a mouse or a rat!'

'I'll make sure that is seen to,' Miss Nightingale said. 'The hospital at Scutari was overrun with rats and I can still remember the letter I wrote to my sister Parthe about them – *Enter me with a lantern in one hand and a broomstick in the other . . . broomstick descends . . . enemy dead . . . slain cast out of hut but unburied.*'

'It must have been terrible!' Beth said, and tried not to laugh as she imagined Miss Nightingale chasing rats with a broomstick.

The lady chuckled.

'There was a time when one of my nurses sat down on her bed and found she'd squashed a whole *nest* of rats. I cannot tell you how grateful I was when a soldier presented us with a small yellow cat to help keep the rats and mice down. That soldier should have been given a medal and the cat should have been given two!'

'Were the rats very big?' Beth asked her and Miss Nightingale nodded.

'Indeed they were – almost as big as Scamp.'

'That's like the rats where we live,' Beth said, and then she closed her mouth quickly at the sight of Miss Nightingale's shocked face.

'Really, dear? You shouldn't be living in a place infested with rats,' she said. 'No wonder your sister is ill. It really isn't good for a sick person to be surrounded by vermin. Rats are so much dirtier than the odd house mouse, you know.'

'It's not so bad,' Beth said. She ignored Miss Nightingale's frown and turned to Scamp instead. 'Let's take your harness off for now.'

As soon as the bandage was removed Scamp hopped up on to the windowsill and looked out at the birds again.

'Next time I come perhaps I could take him outside?' Beth asked.

'I think Scamp would like that very much indeed,' Miss Nightingale smiled and then she winced in pain.

'Are you all right, Miss Nightingale?' Beth asked, hurrying to her.

'It's nothing. Just a slight headache. I think maybe I'll sleep a little now. You can go, Beth. But I would very much appreciate it if you could come back next Saturday and sketch some more of the cats, as well as taking Scamp for his promised walk.'

'I'd like that very much,' Beth said. 'Shall I take Scamp back to the cats' room before I leave?'

'Oh no, let him stay. I like to watch him,' Miss Nightingale said, looking over at the kitten fondly. 'He is good friends with Tom and Topsy, and Scamp's such a funny little thing. He always makes me smile. Oh, and don't forget to sketch your sister, will you?

Why don't you take the smaller sketchbook and some pencils home?' She picked up a book from the bedside table. 'And your sister might find this interesting reading. No need to return it – it's a gift.'

Beth gave Scamp, Tom and Topsy a stroke before she headed downstairs to the waiting carriage.

Chapter 7

When Beth told Iris the match tax wasn't going to happen Iris was over the moon. The two sisters danced around their tiny room singing the marching chant as loudly as they could.

'*Then thirty thousand working girls*
Will know the reason why!'

They kept on singing until someone from the next room started banging on the wall and shouted at them to shut up.

'Miss Nightingale also gave me this book to give to you,' Beth said.

Iris was very good at reading and had always had her head buried in a book when she'd been an assistant teacher in Ireland, but they couldn't afford to have any books of their own since their parents had died.

'*Notes on Nursing*,' Iris read from the cover. She gasped. 'Miss Nightingale wrote this herself! I'll make sure I read it from back to front as quickly as I can and then you can return it to the great lady.'

'Oh no, Miss Nightingale said it didn't need to be returned – it's a gift,' Beth said with a smile. She felt very proud that Miss Florence Nightingale, the great lady with the lamp, had become their friend.

On Sunday Beth tried to make a sketch of Iris and her swollen face while she wasn't looking, but it was too difficult to keep her book hidden.

'Oh, Beth!' Iris cried. 'What are you doing? Why are you drawing me when I look like this? How can you be so cruel? Is it to show to people so they can laugh?'

'Of course not,' Beth said quickly. 'I'd never do something like that! Miss Nightingale thought she might be able to offer some advice if she could only see what your face actually looks like – and where it is swollen.'

'She did?'

Beth nodded. 'If you could tell me a little bit about exactly how it feels, I could let her know that too. Miss Nightingale thinks she may be able to let you know what is actually wrong.'

'I don't need someone else to tell me what I have – I already know!' Iris said as a tear rolled down her swollen face. 'Some of the girls from the factory came to see me. They think I've got phossy jaw and so does Harry. That's why he told me not to come into work!'

Beth's mouth fell open in shock. She shook her head. Phossy jaw was too awful even to think about.

'It starts with a toothache and swelling of the gums, just like I have,' Iris told her.

'You can't have phossy jaw,' Beth said. 'You just can't!'

They both knew it was likely to be a death sentence if she did. Iris's jaw would gradually disintegrate as the disease spread. And even if by some miracle she did survive it, her jaw would never recover.

'I've seen them,' Iris said quietly. 'Match-workers whose faces have been damaged. The factory pays them to stay home so they don't distress the other workers, but they only pay them for thirty weeks and then they don't get taken back on and no other factory will employ them. Even if you live, it's a ticket to the workhouse – or worse.'

'But losing you . . .' Beth said and shuddered.

'Everyone knows it's caused by the white phosphorous we dip the wood into. Dipping all day, every day! There's nowhere to wash our hands and we have to stay and work at the phosphorous bench – even to eat! – or we get our wages docked.'

'You can't have phossy jaw!' Beth exclaimed again. She couldn't lose her sister as well as her mam and da. She remembered Harry and Florence's questions about Iris's face. They must both have wondered whether she had the terrible disease.

'But what if I do?' Iris said miserably. Tears were still rolling out of her bloodshot eyes and over her poor swollen face.

'Let's see what Miss Nightingale says,' Beth told her sister, determined to be practical. 'Open your mouth wide, over by the window, so I can see and draw the inside of it.'

Iris opened her mouth as widely as she could and Beth had a good look inside. She made sure she carefully drew each of Iris's teeth in the sketch and labelled them with a number. Then she spotted something white right at the back of the gums, piercing through a section of gum that looked extremely red and swollen.

'Warr-is-it?' Iris said with her mouth still open.

'Just being careful to get all your teeth in my drawing,' Beth said, labelling that tooth too. But she felt very worried about her sister's red jaw and the white bit at the back.

Iris was so conscious of her swollen face that she refused to go out at all unless she'd fully covered up using their mother's shawl to stop people staring.

'No one's really looking,' Beth tried to reassure her. 'They're too busy with their own lives.'

But Iris didn't believe it. She didn't want to go out any more. All she wanted to do was read Miss Nightingale's book.

When they ran out of food it was Beth who went to the market to buy more. There she met Molly, one of Iris's co-workers from the factory.

'Have you heard there's not going to be a match tax any more?' Molly asked Beth, and when Beth nodded she said, 'It's all thanks to Mister Bryant and Mister May. Harry told us they should have a testimonial fountain, with a great tower to it, built outside Bow Station to celebrate them getting the match tax revoked. Everyone cheered when he suggested it.'

Beth frowned. She'd read Queen Victoria's letter and was sure *that* had been the real reason the tax had been stopped. Nothing to do with Mr Bryant and Mr May at all!

'We're going to donate some of our wages – a little bit every week to pay for it,' Molly added. Beth thought about that coming out of her poor sister's wages.

She bought a loaf of bread and headed home. She didn't want Iris to have phossy jaw and even if by some miracle she didn't have the disease, Beth worried about her going back to work at a factory where she could get it. But she didn't want the two of them to end up in the workhouse either. Once she'd drawn all of Miss Nightingale's cats she wouldn't be needed at 10 South Street and the money from sketching the cats would stop. She tried not to think about that.

When she got home Iris was still engrossed in Miss Nightingale's book. *At this rate*, Beth thought, *she'll finish it in no time*.

'Hurry home as soon as Miss Nightingale's made her diagnosis!' Iris called after her when Beth left in the carriage for number 10 South Street at 8.15 the next Saturday morning.

Beth was glad to find Florence was feeling much stronger than the last time she'd visited and was able to work at her writing desk in the cats' room, her beloved pets around her and little Scamp on the windowsill. When Beth arrived he came racing over to her.

Florence smiled and nodded as she looked through all of Beth's sketches of Iris's face and the inside of her mouth.

Beth watched her anxiously. 'Is it true?' she said, biting her lip. 'Does poor Iris have phossy jaw?'

'On the contrary, my dear, it's just as I'd hoped,' Miss Nightingale said, looking closely at one particular drawing. 'Your sister Iris's jaw does not have the characteristic misshapenness of the phossy jaw sufferer. I'm not a doctor, though I should have liked to be one, but I can say with all certainty it is *not* the dreaded match-factory disease. It's Iris's wisdom teeth trying to push their way through the gums that's causing the problem.'

'Is it serious?' Beth asked her, the relief making her almost light-headed.

'Not nearly as serious as phossy jaw,' Miss Nightingale said. 'And earache is a common symptom. Wisdom teeth are the last to appear and don't usually arrive until a person is between seventeen and twenty-five. How old is your sister?'

'She'll be twenty-three next month.'

Florence nodded. 'Just the age I would expect this to occur. It should all calm down soon, but it may take a few weeks! In the meantime a little oil of cloves should help.' She handed Beth a small brown glass bottle. 'I don't agree with nurses prescribing regular medicine; that should be a doctor or a pharmacist's job,' Miss Nightingale said. 'But I do agree with giving out a herbal medicine like this one because it has been used successfully for centuries and can do little harm but much good.'

'Thank you so much,' Beth said, 'you've been so kind to us. I don't know how I can ever repay you.' She was amazed Florence could spend any time at all thinking of her and Iris when she had so many things of her own to juggle. Beth knew she was dealing with her nursing school and endeavouring to reform the workhouses, while always trying to help the poor and spreading the word about the importance of cleanliness and sanitation.

'I believe you told little Scamp he could go outside on his harness today?' Florence said as she tied the bandage round him.

'Yes – yes, I did,' Beth said.

Scamp raced over to the door, gave a loud *miaow*, sat down and looked over at Beth hopefully.

'Why don't you take him to the park? The daffodils are beautiful and George is there already doing a bit of fishing,' Florence said as she turned back to her work.

As soon as Beth opened the door, the kitten started pulling ahead of her and trying to jump down the stairs.

'Oh no! You'll hurt one of us doing that,' Beth said, and she scooped Scamp up and carried him down the steps. She set him on the floor again once they were in the hallway. 'Now we're safe.'

As they walked along South Street, Scamp looked up at the white-blossomed tree. Small birds still flew in and out of it, but one bird, a big crow, sat right at the top and looked down at him. *Caw!* The crow cawed, but it didn't swoop or try to peck him. Scamp quickened his step and kept his head down just in case.

Beth picked Scamp up again when they reached busy Park Lane. She waited for a gap between the coaches and horse-drawn hansom cabs that were rushing past. And when it was safe she carried the kitten across the road and only then put him down once they'd gone through the wrought-iron gates of Hyde Park.

As soon as his paws touched the grass, Scamp darted from one interesting sniffing spot to another as Beth ran to keep up with him. A squirrel scurried across the grass one way and then another squirrel scurried the other way. Scamp tried to chase one of them and then the other, but the squirrels ran up different tree trunks and stared down at him and Beth.

'Those squirrels are too quick and crafty to be caught by a little kitten,' Beth told Scamp. He looked up at her with his big amber eyes and gave a *miaow* as if he were agreeing with her and Beth laughed.

The park was much busier than when Beth had last been here, with all sorts of people walking around it.

'Fine-looking kitten!' called out a red-faced man sitting on a bench.

'Thanks!' Beth called back as she hurried on.

She couldn't see George anywhere.

A cabbage-white butterfly fluttered past and Beth looked down as Scamp stopped and tilted his head to watch it, entranced. He wanted to run after the pretty creature and Beth, who was trying not to pull too much on the bandage lead, went with him.

Another butterfly fluttered past and Scamp put his paw out and almost danced along as he tried to follow that one instead. The butterfly settled on a daffodil and Scamp sat down to watch it.

'Your kitten looks so sweet,' said a friendly-looking girl wearing a straw hat.

Scamp jumped up and hid behind Beth's legs to stare warily at the girl's King Charles spaniel puppy.

'I don't know if Scamp's ever met a puppy before,' Beth said, looking down at him.

'This is Oscar and he loves cats. We've got three at home and he goes to sleep with them every night. My name's Maude. What's yours?'

'Beth,' Beth told her. 'And this is Scamp. Hello, Oscar!'

The puppy sniffed at Scamp, who came out from behind Beth's legs and sniffed back. Oscar wagged his tail at Scamp, but the kitten didn't wag his tail back.

'Dogs show they're happy by wagging their tails,' Maude said. 'But cats aren't happy if they're wagging their tails wildly – they're annoyed. My mum and dad are naturalists and study animal behaviour, like Charles Darwin, although they're not famous like him. There's a funny quote about cats that they like.' She frowned as she tried to remember it. 'Oh yes! *Cats are a mysterious kind of folk. There is more passing in their minds than we are aware of.*'

Beth laughed. 'Who said that?'

'The Scottish poet, Sir Walter Scott.'

'If that's true about the tails, how do you know when a cat's happy or wants to play?' Beth asked Maude. It would be lovely to know more about how Scamp was feeling.

'Purring's a good sign,' Maude told her with a grin. 'And if a kitten wants to play he'll let you know . . . by playing with you!'

Maude frowned as she looked over Beth's shoulder and saw the red-faced man heading over to them.

'That's a nice-looking kitten you've got there,' he said.

Beth's brow furrowed. She was sure he'd already said that. 'A Persian pedigree, if I'm not mistaken. Worth a bob or two, no doubt.'

The two girls looked at each other, not at all sure about the man.

'We have to be going,' Maude told him, but the next moment the man snatched Scamp's bandage harness right out of Beth's hands and ran off with the kitten.

'No!' Beth cried.

The two girls and Oscar ran as fast as they could after the man who'd stolen Scamp, but his legs were a lot longer than theirs and he was much quicker.

'Thief! Cat thief!' yelled Maude as they ran. Park-goers looked round, but didn't come to help.

Ahead of them Beth watched poor Scamp being half swung along by the bandages, unable to get away.

'Help!' Beth shouted as loudly as she could as the man got further and further away. He disappeared into the wooded area, Scamp still dangling from his harness.

Just then a boy holding a long fishing rod came running up. 'Whatever is the matter?' he cried. It was George – to Beth's great relief. Now he could help them save Scamp!

'A little kitten has been stolen! The thief's gone into those woods,' Maude told him.

George looked at Beth. 'Not Scamp?'

She nodded miserably.

A policeman was heading towards them. Usually Beth would have done her best to avoid him, but George had no such fears and ran straight over.

'Miss Florence Nightingale's pedigree kitten's been stolen,' he told the policeman. He pointed to the woods where Scamp had been taken.

The policeman immediately blew on his shrill whistle to alert other officers as he ran into the woods with Beth, Maude, Oscar and George. In no time at all they were joined by three other policemen who'd heard the whistle.

Scamp was sore from being carried along by the bandage harness and scratched from the prickly bush the thief had pulled him through.

But finally, deep in the woods, where the embers of a campfire were still glowing, the red-faced thief dropped the kitten on the ground and then collapsed by the dying fire. Two other thieves came out from their hiding place in the trees to join him.

'What you got there then, Frank?' said the first one.

'Could hear you thundering through the woods like a great bull in a china shop,' the second one told him.

'Got this,' Frank said, pulling at Scamp's bandage harness.

Scamp tried to scratch Frank with his tiny paws.

'Oh no you don't!' Frank told him.

'A cat?'

'A kitten,' Frank said as Scamp's amber eyes looked up at him. 'A very rare male calico.'

'What's the big deal about that? I thought you were going to steal us some money!'

'It is money – or it will be. This kitten's a pedigree Persian. Worth a lot of money to his owner.'

'So we're holding it for ransom?'

Frank nodded. 'That's the plan.'

'Good one. Here, we've got a sack we can keep it in, in case any peelers come snooping.'

But as the thief opened the sack and Frank tried to stuff the kitten into it Scamp heard Beth's voice calling him.

'Scamp! Scamp!'

The kitten twisted and wriggled, scratching and biting at Frank's hand like a wildcat.

'Yeowch!' Frank shouted.

He only loosened his grip for a millisecond, but it was long enough for Scamp to escape. He landed on the soft leafy ground, rolled over and a second later was up and running through the woods with three thieves racing after him.

Scamp leapt over the small bushes and twigs in his way. The thieves just ploughed through them.

'Stop that cat!' they shouted to each other.

Scamp saw Beth and leapt straight into her grasp. The thieves skidded to a halt as they spotted the police, but it was too late. George tripped one of them up with his fishing rod and the other two ran straight into the arms of the law.

Oscar looked up at Scamp and wagged his tail. Scamp put out his paw to the puppy and gave a *miaow*.

'Thank goodness we got you back!' Maude said to Scamp. 'Well done with that fishing-rod swing!' she told George.

'This is George,' Beth told her.

'Nice to meet you, George,' Maude grinned. 'Come on, Oscar, we'd better be getting home. We're late already! Goodbye, Beth!'

'Thank you for helping us,' Beth called after her as they ran off. She was very glad Maude and Oscar had been there too.

Beth hugged Scamp to her and kissed the top of his furry head. 'I'm so relieved that we found you,' she said as the three of them headed back to number 10 South Street. She was feeling a bit shaky and Scamp was trembling in her arms.

'Lucky I was there,' George said.

'Lucky indeed,' Beth agreed.

'I was fishing,' George said, swinging his rod, 'but I didn't catch any fish – just a kitten thief!' And he laughed and laughed at his own joke as they went up the steps of Miss Nightingale's house.

Beth joined in too, but with relief because she had been truly very scared.

Scamp curled up on Beth's lap and she stroked him while George, with shining eyes, told Miss Nightingale everything that had happened.

'Lucky I was there, Miss Nightingale. I swung my fishing rod and tripped one of them up. I should be Scamp's bodyguard – and Beth's!'

Beth was about to say she didn't need a bodyguard, but Miss Nightingale caught her eye and gave a gentle smile. This was George's moment.

'Lucky you were there, George,' she agreed as Scamp looked up at her with his beautiful amber eyes and purred.

Chapter 8

Iris was waiting outside the house when Edward dropped Beth back. She still had their mother's shawl wrapped round her face so no one could see her jaw.

'See you next Saturday, Beth,' Edward told her as Beth hopped out.

'Bye, Edward,' Beth said.

'So what's Miss Nightingale's verdict?' Iris asked her as soon as the horse had clip-clopped away.

'*Not* phossy jaw!' Beth said and Iris gave a loud sigh of relief.

'What is it, then?' she asked. 'It's very painful and it looks terrible. And although my earache's not as bad as it was, it's definitely still there.'

'Miss Nightingale thinks it's your wisdom teeth coming through. This should help,' Beth said and she offered Iris the small brown glass bottle the lady had given to her.

Iris read the label. '*Oil of cloves*. Do I just take a swig of it or do I need to mix it with water?'

'I think you dab a little on the sore area,' Beth told her.

Iris pulled the cork from the bottle and dabbed away. 'Oh! It feels like it's numbing my gum already,' she said. 'The pain isn't so bad.'

'Miss Nightingale said it might take a few weeks to get completely better. But it should calm down once the wisdom teeth at the back of your mouth have come through. I think you might be nearly there, though, Iris, because I saw something white poking through your gums at the very back of your mouth. Miss Nightingale said it was definitely a tooth. If you'd been a baby I'd have said you were teething!'

Iris started laughing so hard that tears ran down her face. 'Just teething!' she cried. 'Only teething!' Then Beth hugged her as she let out a huge sob – the prospect of having phossy jaw had been too awful to contemplate and now it was nearly all over.

Iris had almost finished Miss Nightingale's book, *Notes on Nursing*, and couldn't wait to start implementing some of the advice inside it. She'd already moved Beth's drawing to a spot on the wall and opened the window so they got more fresh air.

'The window was so stiff I don't think it can have been opened in years. And tomorrow I'm going to scrub our room from top to bottom!' she told Beth.

'And I'll help,' Beth said. She couldn't wait to tell her sister all about the adventure in the park.

It was hard work cleaning the whole room, even though it was very small, especially as they had to keep getting water from the communal pump. The house had no pipes, so there was no fresh water running through it.

As they worked, Iris related snippets and helpful hints from Miss Nightingale's book.

'Miss Nightingale says a nurse should take care always to put things in the same place so she can find them easily,' Iris said to Beth.

The sisters didn't have many things to lose, but it was still sometimes hard to find them when they were in a rush.

'Oh, and she said a small pet animal is often an excellent companion for the sick and for long chronic cases especially. Do you think that's why she has so many cats?'

'Maybe,' Beth said. Miss Nightingale certainly did love her cats and she was often ill. 'She said she's never been quite right since she came back from the Crimea. Miss Nightingale thinks it's because she drank some infected goat's milk.'

Iris was nodding. 'Miss Nightingale says in her book that even water can be infected and we should never drink any that isn't perfectly clear and without taste or smell.'

By the evening their room was spotless – in fact, it was almost starting to look like a home.

'Much better!' Iris said, and Beth agreed. Mrs Brompton, who lived downstairs and owned the house, knocked on the door of their room.

Iris ran and grabbed the shawl to cover her face and Beth opened the door.

'Well, haven't you two been working hard,' Mrs Brompton said as she came inside and looked around.

'Many hands make light work,' Beth quipped.

'That's another thing Miss Nightingale said in her book,' Iris observed. Her voice sounded muffled behind the shawl. *'Every nurse ought to be careful to wash her hands very frequently during the day. If her face too, so much the better.'*

'You all right, Iris?' Mrs Brompton asked her.

'Yes, just a pain in my gums where my wisdom teeth are coming through,' Iris told her.

'And how come you're quoting Miss Florence Nightingale?'

Iris grabbed her copy of *Notes on Nursing* to show her, eagerly talking about all that she'd learnt.

*

Miss Florence Nightingale was in her bed and in a lot of pain the next time Beth visited, but the first thing she asked was, 'And how's your sister now? Did the clove oil help at all?'

'A little better, thank you,' Beth told her. Florence tried to get herself into a more comfortable position in the bed, her face grimacing in pain. Beth helped to put more pillows behind her. 'The clove oil definitely helped Iris's teething and she's enthralled by your book. In fact, she hasn't stopped reading it since I gave it to her and is already implementing your good advice. Our window is now open day and night – although I'm not sure how fresh the air is – and it's noisy from the adjacent roofs where the homeless boys go to sleep.'

'But it's better than having a window all shut up and stagnant air within the room,' Miss Nightingale told her. 'I'm very pleased your sister is following my advice. She seems like a very wise young woman as well as a wonderful sister to you.'

'Oh, she is,' Beth agreed, 'and a hard worker too, although she's not allowed to go back to work at the factory until her face is completely unswollen. The factory is even paying her to stay home!'

'Are they, indeed,' Florence said, her lips pursed.

'We scrubbed our room from top to bottom last Sunday and it's looking as bright and fresh as a new penny,' Beth continued.

Florence smiled. 'Fresh air and good nutrition, those are the important things, as well as sanitation, of course, that made all the difference to our soldiers in the Crimea. Did you know the barracks hospital at Scutari where my nurses and I were placed was built over an open sewer, of all things? And the *smell*! It doesn't even bear thinking about. My time there is in the past. But the infection, disease and death that insanitary conditions bring about – well, those are ongoing and I intend to do everything in my power to stop them!'

While Beth worked on a drawing of Topsy and Tom playing together on the bed, Miss Nightingale read and wrote letters. Beth thought how the lady always had an awful lot of letters to read. Not just from England, but from all over the world, judging by the different stamps the envelopes had on them.

'Many people write to me asking for advice,' Miss Nightingale told her. 'But lots of the letters are from people needing money too. I help when I can.' Scamp hopped on to the bed to join Tom and Topsy, and she stroked him. 'Unfortunately, there are so many requests I simply can't help everyone. I wish I could do more.' She shook her head. 'I just wish I could do more.'

'You already do such a lot,' Beth said as she added Scamp to the Tom and Topsy drawing. 'More than anyone I know.'

Florence shook her head. 'I will never forget my tour of the Marylebone workhouse in the late eighteen forties. The wretched, desperate conditions broke my heart. Thank goodness after the Crimean war I was able to place some of my first Nightingale-trained nurses there to help. And my nurses went to the Liverpool workhouse too. Dear Agnes Jones was one of my very best – she was made the superintendent there. Under her guidance it became a safe haven for famine immigrants from Ireland. Typhus and cholera were rampant, but as always, once the hospital was clean within its walls, the death rate went down. Agnes worked tirelessly to help others.

She overworked as others underwork. I looked upon her as one of the most valuable lives in England and her passing as one of the saddest. I'll never forget her.'

Florence dabbed at her eyes with a lace handkerchief and for a moment Beth wasn't sure what to do. But then she went over to the bed, sat down and put her hand on Florence's. The three kittens came to join them and Scamp climbed on Miss Nightingale's pillow, purring.

'So many good people,' the lady said, 'and so sad when they leave us. The writer Mister Charles Dickens and I worked together to press for further improvements to the workhouse before he passed away last year. His stories so eloquently showed the lives of poor people for what they are. No different from us in all the important ways. Dear Charles pushed for free schooling for all and would be very pleased with Parliament for passing the Education Act last year. I tried to give the soldiers intellectual stimulation while they were recuperating during the Crimea. His stories went down very well. Have you read any of Dickens's work?'

Beth shook her head. Although she thought Iris may have done. She'd always been reading when they'd lived in Ireland.

'Well, then you're in for a treat!' Miss Nightingale said, pulling copies of *Oliver Twist* and *A Christmas Carol* from the bookshelf behind her and handing them to Beth. 'Your sister will probably enjoy them too. Oh – I almost forgot *Great Expectations*.' And she pulled another book from the shelf.

George brought in two cups of tea and some freshly made scones and jam for Miss Nightingale and Beth, along with a little fish for Scamp, Topsy and Tom.

'Mother's just made these scones so they're still warm,' he said. He looked over at Beth's latest sketch of Tom, Topsy and Scamp playing. 'Not bad,' he said grudgingly.

As soon as Scamp had finished eating his fish, he hopped back on to the windowsill. Today there were sparrows and blackbirds, starlings and squirrels to watch.

'Give the birds these few crumbs, will you?' Florence asked Beth when she'd had enough of her scone. 'I can't manage any more and I do so love to see the birds pecking away outside my window. Be careful little Scamp doesn't squeeze his way through the window to join them, though!'

When Beth had fed the birds, been given a look of reproach by Scamp and returned to the bedside, Florence said, 'I do hope you have good nourishing hot food to keep you and your sister's strength up at home?'

Beth was surprised at the question and Florence's kindness in thinking of them when she herself was in pain. She told the lady that they ate as well as they could, although it wasn't always easy without any running water or an oven to cook hot food in.

'If we want hot food we have to buy whatever's being sold on the open-air hot food stalls.'

'So you don't even have a fire?' Miss Nightingale asked, and Beth shook her head. Rooms with fires cost a lot more and, anyway, they wouldn't have been able to pay for the coal or wood or even the matches to light it. The elderly lady sighed and rested her head on the pillows. 'How on earth are people supposed to manage?' she said. 'How is anyone in your situation to be expected to survive, let alone flourish?'

Beth stroked Scamp because there was really nothing she could say other than that they, like most people they knew, survived as best they could.

'A wonderful chef called Alexis Soyer accompanied me in May eighteen fifty-five when I travelled to Balaclava during the Crimean war,' Florence told Beth.

'Is that who Soyer the grey cat's named after?' Beth said, and Florence nodded.

'With us were four hundred and twenty soldiers who were to return to their regiments and fight again on the battlefront. Soyer was a truly amazing man with such a good heart. Before he went to the Crimea he'd previously helped people affected by the famine in Ireland and invented the soup kitchen to feed the hungry. And when he arrived he created wonderful recipes using the army rations to make excellent soups and stews. He insisted on having soldiers who could be trained as cooks permanently allocated to the kitchens and he invented ovens to bake bread and biscuits and a Scutari teapot that made and kept tea hot for fifty men!'

'Fifty!' Beth said. 'That must have been a huge teapot.'

Florence chuckled. 'He was amazing. Did you know he even cooked breakfast for two thousand people at Queen Victoria's coronation?'

Beth shook her head because of course she hadn't known. Sometimes Miss Nightingale seemed to forget they existed in two different worlds.

'We both came down with a terrible fever at Balaclava,' Florence added. 'My hair was cropped in an attempt to quell the malady and I had to wear a black handkerchief under my white lace cap.'

'Thank goodness you survived!' Beth said as Scamp came over now the birds had eaten all the crumbs. He jumped up on to Miss

Nightingale's bed to join Tom and Topsy and she gave him a stroke.

'While I was there my sister Parthe sent me a story about a pet owl I used to have called Athena, along with a picture of the two of us.' Miss Nightingale took a piece of paper from her bedside cabinet and showed Beth the drawing of herself and a very small owl that was sitting on top of a dresser and staring out from the picture.

'Oh, he's sweet!' Beth said.

'And very small,' Florence told her. 'Smaller than you are now, Scamp. When I was younger, my sister and I went on wonderful tours of so many places. In eighteen fifty we were in Italy and I rescued that tiny creature. It's called a little owl – *Athene noctua* is the scientific name. Oh, Beth, the places I've seen! When I'm lying in my bed I think of them all. Little Athena saw many places too.'

George came in with the post on a silver tray and Miss Nightingale picked up an embossed envelope, opened it and then frowned.

'Oh, I really don't feel at all well enough to go to the opening,' she said. 'I can't possibly attend.'

'What is it?' Beth asked, and George stopped at the door and turned back.

'Queen Victoria is opening the new Saint Thomas's Hospital in June,' the lady replied. 'My Nightingale Nurses' training school will be moved from the old Saint Thomas's to there. I wonder, though . . .' She trailed off, thinking.

'What, Florence?' Beth asked her.

'The public are welcome to go into the building and look around after the queen has opened it and left. Do you think you could possibly go and look for me?'

'Me?' Beth said, swallowing hard. 'You want me to go?' She could hardly believe Miss Florence Nightingale was asking her to do something so important.

'I'll go for you, Miss Nightingale,' George said eagerly.

'I'm afraid not, George,' she said, turning back to Beth. 'It's on a Wednesday, so George won't be able to go with you as he'll be at school. But maybe, if she hasn't returned to work at the factory yet, your sister Iris might be interested in going?'

'I'm sure she would,' Beth said.

'Good,' said Miss Nightingale. 'I'll ask Edward to collect you both in the coach.'

Iris's wisdom tooth had finally come through and her face was back to its unswollen self just a few weeks later.

'Glad to see you without a rag covering your smile,' Edward told her as he helped Iris and Beth into the coach.

'Looks like it's going to rain,' Beth said as Edward stopped the coach among the host of others lined up around St Thomas's new hospital next to the Thames. The grey clouds in the sky looked very heavy.

'Come on, Beth,' Iris said, opening the carriage door. 'A spot of rain never hurt us.'

Hand in hand the sisters ran to find a good spot to watch the queen's arrival from and as it turned out it didn't rain at all. The clouds disappeared and there was glorious sunshine by the time Queen Victoria arrived just before noon, dressed all in black, with white flowers in her hair. She was accompanied by a squadron of the Household Cavalry.

Beth and Iris watched in awe as the queen and other members of the royal family entered

St Thomas's, after which a blast of trumpets indicated that Her Majesty had formally opened the hospital; then the 'Old Hundredth' was sung.

'Time for us to have a look around now and report back to Miss Nightingale!' Iris said as they watched the royal coaches leaving a little while later.

'It's amazing,' Beth said as she stared at the massive, magnificent hospital close to the edge of the River Thames. 'And to think Miss Nightingale helped to plan it.'

They wandered around the ornamental grounds that had been designed for convalescent patients to spend time in. There were gravel paths to walk down and flower beds in full bloom.

Inside the hospital, the wards were as neat and sweet-smelling as could be.

'How wonderful to work as a nurse in a hospital like this one,' Iris said.

'I heard that Queen Victoria named one of the wards *Victoria* and another of them *Albert*,' Edward told them when they got back to the coach.

'Let's go and tell Miss Nightingale all about it,' Beth said excitedly.

Florence was lying in her bed when they got back to South Street, but she ordered tea for them all.

'Tell me everything,' she said.

At first Iris was too overawed at meeting the great lady to say anything, but as Miss Nightingale asked her opinion of the wards and the hospital Iris forgot to be nervous. Her eyes shone as she told Miss Nightingale how wonderful the hospital was and how lucky any woman would be to work as a nurse there. Beth looked on, smiling.

'I didn't want it to be built so close to the Thames,' Miss Nightingale said. 'I do worry about disease coming from the river. As I mentioned to you before, the barracks hospital at Scutari was a nightmare. The soldiers would have been better off not going to a hospital at all than going there – cholera, dysentery, typhoid and malaria, not to mention the rats and the unsanitary nature of the place. When I realized the place had been built over that sewer, I sent a desperate plea to *The Times* newspaper, begging the government to produce a solution. And they did.'

'What was the solution, Miss Nightingale?' Iris asked.

'Isambard Kingdom Brunel –' the lady started to say, but Beth interrupted excitedly.

'Is Izzy the cat named after him?'

Florence chuckled. 'Yes. Isambard Kingdom Brunel designed a prefabricated hospital that could be built in England and then shipped ready to be erected in the Crimea. He did a fantastic job and incorporated all the necessities of hygiene that had been so sadly lacking before and cost many men their lives. Now we had sanitation, ventilation, proper drainage and even some basic temperature controls. It was wonderful.'

'How many soldiers could it care for?' Iris asked.

'It treated thirteen hundred patients,' Florence told her. 'It was really very clever, a series of magnificent hospital huts. Each hut, or ward, could house fifty patients and there were sixty wards. I was only sad that I was not allowed to manage the new hospital, but I am very glad for all the lives it saved. *The Times* fund that was set up to help the wounded soldiers assisted in many ways. The public were so generous in their support and supplied the soldiers with clothes, bedding and food. I truly believe most people try to do good, but sometimes they need steering in the right direction.'

The tea was brought in and Miss Nightingale told the sisters that she wanted to see them both eat a lot.

Iris squeezed Beth's hand. There was far more food than they would usually have eaten in a whole day.

'What a pretty blue design,' Iris said when she was given her plate.

'It's called the Willow Pattern,' Florence told her. 'It originated in China and has been popular in England for over a hundred years.'

'The tea's extra delicious with sugar in it,' Beth told her sister, dropping a few cubes into Iris's cup.

She could see by Iris's smile when she sipped that she agreed.

Even though they were both very hungry, they didn't forget the good manners their mother had taught them, and thanked Florence very much.

Scamp was given a little dish of rice pudding as it was almost five o'clock. The other pets were having theirs in the cats' room, but Scamp liked to be wherever Beth was.

'I'm so pleased you're not suffering with your wisdom teeth any more,' Miss Nightingale told Iris. 'And Beth told me you found my little book, *Notes on Nursing*, a help.'

Iris nodded around a mouthful of scone.

'And do you think one day you might possibly like to become a nurse?' Miss Nightingale asked – and Iris only just managed not to choke as she swallowed the scone. 'I'm in charge of selecting our new probationers,' Miss Nightingale continued, 'and you, my dear, took on board and then put all of my nursing suggestions into effect. You're just the sort of trainee nurse I would want at Saint Thomas's.'

Iris looked like she could hardly believe her ears.

'Really, Miss Nightingale?' she said.

'Yes, my dear. If you think it would suit? You'd have to live in the nurses' quarters at the hospital, but Beth could come and live here, so you wouldn't have to worry about her.'

'I would like that more than anything in the world!' Iris exclaimed happily.

'And you, Beth. Would you be happy living here?' Florence asked her.

'Yes, I would!' Beth said, beaming, as Scamp finished his rice pudding and hopped up into her lap.

Chapter 9

When Edward came to pick Beth up on Saturday morning he brought with him two carpetbags, one for each of the sisters.

'Miss Nightingale said you'd need this when you go to train at Saint Thomas's Hospital,' he said, giving one of the bags to Iris. 'And she said you'd need this one to pack your belongings in when you come to live at South Street,' he told Beth.

*

As soon as Beth walked into the cats' room at number 10, Scamp ran over to her and almost launched himself on to her dress. She scooped him up in her arms and hugged him.

'I thought you might like the attic room when you come to live here,' Florence said. 'It has a window with a small balcony for when Scamp comes to visit. I suspect he may be wanting to do that a lot!'

Beth ran up the two flights of stairs to the bright room at the top of the house with Scamp in her arms. He snuggled beside her as she lay down on the bed and stared at the ceiling with a huge smile on her face. Miss Nightingale had even arranged for a small vase containing yellow roses to be placed on the bedside table.

'This is just perfect!' she told Scamp as he ran down the bed and jumped on to the windowsill.

*

When Beth and Scamp came back downstairs Miss Nightingale was at her writing desk working on a circular graph.

'What's that?' Beth asked.

'It's called a polar diagram,' the lady told her, 'and it's a clear way of showing recorded facts so everyone can understand them. Maths is the thing, Beth. Statistics prove the truth.' She pulled out a finished printed diagram similar to the one she was working on from a desk drawer. 'This is a record of how soldiers died during the Crimean War. It makes me sad to look at it because I think of all the wasted lives that could have been saved if we'd only realized that lack of sanitation was causing more deaths than actual wounds. Sadly, it is now too late to change the past – unlike the present and future, which I will do everything in my power to improve!'

'How long did it take for you to travel from England to the Crimea?' Beth asked. She tried to picture where it was, but her knowledge of geography was very limited.

Florence showed her on a globe.

'Thirty-eight nurses and my housekeeper, Mrs Clarke, as well as Mister and Mrs Bracebridge, left England on the twenty-first of October eighteen fifty-four,' she said, pointing to Britain on the globe. 'On the twenty-seventh of October, we had to travel on a mail boat called the *Vectis*. It was overrun with cockroaches and I felt so ill I couldn't wait for it to be over! We arrived in Constantinople on the fourth of November, two weeks after we'd set off.' As she spoke she traced her finger across the globe past Belgium and through Germany and Vienna, in Austria, and across the whole continent of Europe.

'Such a long way,' Beth said, and she couldn't keep the envy from her voice. 'You must have seen so much.' She loved hearing or reading about the great explorers and voyagers like Mr Charles Darwin. It must be wonderful knowing you were making permanent records of the places you'd seen and the creatures you'd found.

Scamp came over and pushed his head under Beth's hand for a stroke and Miss Nightingale smiled as she watched him.

'You're going to be very happy once Beth's living here too, little one,' she said to the kitten.

'And I'm going to be very happy as well,' Beth said as George brought in the newspapers and then went to fetch them some tea.

So far Beth had drawn lots of sketches of Scamp and a few of Tom and Topsy.

'Your turn today, Aggy,' she told the black-and-white cat.

Aggy was very interested in the colourful toy George had made using some of the feathers from his fishing tackle. She chased after the plaything when Beth jiggled it and tried to pounce when Beth pulled the string George had tied the feathers to. When Aggy finally caught her prey, she lay down with the feather toy and Beth began to draw her.

'Oh, fancy that,' Florence remarked as she turned the pages of the newspaper. 'The queen's nephew, who fought in the Crimean War, has sculpted a terracotta bust of Mrs Mary Seacole and it's to be exhibited at the National Gallery next year. Mary stayed with us at the hospital in Scutari overnight before she went on to the battlefront at Balaclava. She did a great deal of good for the poor soldiers there. I contributed to a fund that was set up to help her after the war. But, Beth, you really should go to the National Gallery, and not just to see the sculptures. There are so many wonderful works of art there; I'm sure you will leave feeling utterly inspired.'

'I should love to go,' Beth said.

'Then you must!' said Florence firmly. 'You could take George or your sister with you.' But then she was distracted by something else in the newspaper. 'Well, I never . . .'

'What is it, Florence?' Beth asked, redrawing her sketch of Aggy's ear because it hadn't looked quite right.

'There's going to be a cat exhibition at the Crystal Palace tomorrow. The first ever cat show in Britain and they're calling for competitors. Beth, I think we should enter, don't you?'

'Yes, indeed,' Beth agreed, wondering how this was to happen, as Florence almost never went out.

'Of course I can't go myself,' Florence said, echoing Beth's thoughts. 'There'd be far too many newspapermen there and you know I can't abide the fuzz-buzz. But you could go and draw sketches of the event for me, so it will feel almost like I've been there too.'

George came in with two cups of tea on a tray.

'Only I don't want you to go alone. You'd better take George with you!' Miss Nightingale said.

'With her where, Miss Nightingale?' George said.

'The Crystal Palace . . . the first ever cat show!' Beth told him with a grin.

'Oh, and you'll need a cat to enter . . .' Florence said. She looked over at Scamp in his favourite place on the windowsill. 'I think I know one who'd be more than happy to go with you, don't you?'

'Yes!' Beth laughed.

At the sound of her laughter Scamp looked over and gave a flick of his tail.

*

The next day, with Scamp wearing a new harness made from white ribbons, Beth and George set off in the carriage for the cat show.

'Can any sort of cat be entered?' Edward asked when he dropped them off. 'I've got a beautiful cat at home, but it isn't a pedigree.'

'Oh yes, all cats are welcome,' Beth told him as Scamp snuggled into her neck and George strode eagerly ahead of them through the glass and iron doors of the magnificent building.

The room in which the cat show was being held contained lots of cats in cages with people walking around pointing and looking at them. Beth didn't think Scamp would like being enclosed like that, so she carried him with them instead.

Scamp stared through the bars at the other fifty-six cats that had been entered. Some of them had cards pinned to their cages with

Highly Commended or *First, Second* or *Third Place* written on them. There were classes for the best of different breeds and novelty classes for the biggest and smallest cats, as well as one for the best-behaved cat on a lead.

'Scamp should enter that!' George said, and Beth nodded.

She thought the cats looked very comfortable sitting on cushions in their cages and smiled to herself when she heard one man tell another, 'They borrowed those cages from the Pigeon Society.'

Scamp was very interested in the other cats, although some of them hissed at him.

'I think you-know-who would be interested in a drawing of this cat and her kittens,' Beth said. They were careful not to mention Miss Nightingale's name because she didn't want any attention from the newspapermen. Beth handed Scamp to George and took out her sketchbook to draw a cat with seven toes, along with her two kittens that also had seven toes.

'I like how you capture the details and label the information,' a voice behind her said, and when Beth looked up, she saw a bearded man with piercing blue-grey eyes and a twinkling smile. She was sure he looked familiar, but she couldn't quite place him.

'I could have done with a second artist like you in the Galapagos Islands,' the man added. 'Meticulousness and precision are what I look for in a good draughtsman – or woman!'

And now Beth realized who he was – Mr Charles Darwin! She was too awestruck to speak.

'Have you drawn the fearsome Scottish wildcat yet?' he asked her.

And when Beth shook her head, still not able to say a word, he continued. 'It's a sight to see.'

And he pointed towards the cage containing the beast.

George and Scamp followed Beth as she headed over to it.

The Scottish wildcat's wrinkled yellow face snarled at the three of them.

'Oh, the poor thing's lost a paw,' Beth said. It only had three paws and she thought it was no wonder it looked so cross. It must have been terrified of the crowds of people coming into the exhibition and staring at it.

Scamp looked at the angry cat and then tucked himself further into George's arms.

Soon it was time for the Best-behaved Cat on a Lead contest in the show ring.

'Do you want to show Scamp or shall I?' Beth asked George.

'I'll do it,' George said, and he carried Scamp over to the other dozen cats on leads that were already waiting with their owners in the ring.

Beth sat down on a bench close by to watch.

Scamp sniffed at a fluffy soft grey Persian kitten with blue eyes. It was on a purple velvet lead.

'No, Lilac,' her lady owner said. 'No playing now.'

Lilac stretched out her purple paw pad to Scamp, but the lady pulled her back so she couldn't reach him.

The kitten looked so pretty that Beth started to sketch her.

Most of the other cats in the ring had ribbon leads like Scamp, but none of them had a ribbon harness. Some of them wore small dog leads and collars. One caramel-coloured cat with black ears had a long silk scarf tied round its neck that it kept trying to bite and scratch.

'No, Sheba, leave it alone,' her owner said wearily.

A ginger cat arched its back and hissed at Scamp.

'Really, Tiger – that's no way to behave,' its owner scolded.

Beth kept drawing the cats as each of the entrants was given a number and lined up. Lilac was in front of Scamp and Tiger was behind him.

The chief judge blew a whistle and the band began to play a marching tune as the cats circled the ring on their leads.

Some of the animals, Beth thought as she watched them, were obviously used to being on a lead, but others weren't at all sure about being pulled along on their collars, and tried to run off.

'No, Sheba!' cried the lady holding the caramel cat with the silk-scarf lead. But Sheba didn't listen as she slipped out of the scarf and escaped into the crowd of spectators. 'Sheba – come back now!' her owner cried, running after her.

As the lady ran, her long skirt accidentally brushed against Tiger and the cat gave a yowl. He raked his claws at Scamp, who bumped into Lilac as he jumped back to avoid Tiger.

In hardly a moment the cat march had turned into cat chaos. Beth was drawing as fast as she could to capture the pandemonium as cats got themselves tangled round owners' legs and women's long skirts, and one man fell over and a cat jumped on top of his head.

George started laughing so hard he was doubled over. But the next moment Scamp broke free from his hands and jumped on top of Beth's sketchbook.

'It's all right,' she said, stroking the kitten. 'I expect you were frightened, but everything's fine.'

'That mischievous kitten's the one that started it,' the chief judge said, pointing at Scamp.

'No, he didn't!' George said, outraged at the false accusation. 'It was *him*.' He pointed to Tiger and his owner.

'It most certainly was not!' said Tiger's owner angrily. 'It was *her*.' And he pointed at Sheba being carried back into the ring by her dishevelled owner.

The chief judge looked at all of them in turn, a frown on his face.

Beth beckoned to George as she stood up with Scamp in her arms. They didn't want to draw too much attention to themselves in case the judge asked who actually owned Scamp.

'Never mind, Scamp,' Beth said as George joined them and they headed back into the crowd of spectators. Behind them, the band began playing the cat march once again.

'Scamp could have won the Best-behaved Cat on a Lead Contest easily,' George said, looking wistfully over his shoulder.

'I know,' Beth said. 'but it was too risky.'

Scamp licked Beth's face with his raspy tongue and she laughed.

Just then, a boy handed George a paper handbill.

'It says there's going to be a second cat show in the autumn,' George told Beth.

'I'm not surprised,' Beth said. The cat show was now heaving with spectators. 'They should have held it over more than one day so everyone didn't have to come at the same time!'

Just before they left the Crystal Palace, they stopped to look at two Siamese cats and Beth gave Scamp to George so she could quickly draw the soft fawn-coloured creatures. There were so many people that her arm was jogged several times as she sketched.

Eventually, just as they were leaving the cat show, they passed a cage containing a cat with no tail.

'It says on the card that it's from the Isle of Man and called a Manx cat, or stubbin, and they're born without tails,' Beth said.

George and Scamp stopped beside the cage of a very large cat with a first prize ribbon pinned to the bars.

'He won it for being the biggest cat here,' George noted.

'Four times the size of you, Scamp,' Beth told Scamp as she took the kitten from George and they returned to Edward and the waiting carriage.

Miss Nightingale was very interested in the drawings Beth had done of the show and agreed that to have spent the day locked in a cage in such a crowded place would not have been good for Scamp.

'I'm glad you went, though; it looks like it was a fascinating experience and adds to your portfolio of drawings,' she said.

'I can draw just as well as she can,' George said sullenly. 'I don't understand the fuss about Beth's drawings.'

Florence's bright eyes looked at him sharply.

'Can you draw, George? I'd love to see some of your sketches, if what you say is true.'

George nodded, although now he looked a bit embarrassed.

'I look forward to it,' Miss Nightingale told him.

'Yes, Miss Nightingale,' said George, but the way he said it made Beth sure he was fibbing.

'Why did you say that to Miss Nightingale?' she asked him when they were alone.

George looked down at his shoes. 'I don't know. Miss Nightingale's always making such a big fuss of you. Much more than she ever does of me!'

'That's no reason to fib to her,' Beth told him. 'Have you even got any sketches?' She'd never seem him drawing.

George shook his head and looked sheepish.

'Could you show me how?' he asked her.

Beth rolled her eyes. 'I'll try,' she said.

At first George found it hard to copy exactly what he saw and learn about perspectives and viewpoints. But Beth said so long as he practised he would get the idea – and one thing about George was that he did practise . . . a lot.

Miss Nightingale was very impressed with all the effort he put in and suggested Beth and he went to Regent's Park Zoological Gardens to practise their drawing some more.

'You'll find hundreds of animals to draw there, although I'm afraid Scamp will not be allowed through the gates.'

Scamp gave a *miaow* and Florence replied to him as if he'd spoken.

'Well, we don't want you becoming one of the exhibits, do we?'

'No, we don't,' Beth laughed.

Edward dropped Beth and George off at the gates to the Regent's Park Zoological Gardens. They both had their sketchbooks with them. Beth thought the animals looked rather sad in their cages and she was glad Scamp would never become one of the exhibits.

'Oh, look!' Beth said as she stopped by the owls' display. '*Athene noctua*,' she read.

'What about it?' George asked, staring at the small bird.

'It's the same sort of owl that Miss Nightingale used to have,' Beth told him. The one in the picture the lady's sister Parthe had drawn wasn't very detailed, although Beth had thought the drawing of Florence herself standing next to the Little Owl was wonderful. The creature blinked at her and Beth pulled out her pencils and started to sketch.

'Oh,' remarked George – and went off to draw one of the vultures in a nearby cage instead.

Chapter 10

Beth waited outside the huge gates of the Bryant and May match factory while Iris went inside to say goodbye. She was very relieved that her sister wasn't going to be working there any more.

'Harry told me he was glad I didn't have phossy jaw,' Iris said when she came out again. 'And the factory girls cheered when they heard I was escaping the daily grind of match life.'

Now Iris was going off to train as a nurse at St Thomas's Hospital and Beth was going to live at South Street, there was no point in keeping their shabby room any more.

'Well, I won't miss this mouldy old space!' Iris said as they packed their few belongings into the carpetbags Miss Nightingale had given them.

'Me, neither,' Beth agreed, but she did think the room was much nicer since they'd given it a proper clean. And living in it was far better than sleeping out on the roofs like some of the boys who went to Dr Barnardo's ragged school. They called the places they slept roof-lays and said it was much safer than sleeping on the street because there was no traffic and also there was a little warmth from the buildings below.

'The peelers don't bother you and no one steals your stuff up there,' one of the boys had told her.

Iris put her arm round Beth's shoulder and gave her a squeeze as a tear slipped down her face.

'I don't suppose I'll miss our room, but I will miss seeing *you* every day very much indeed,' Beth said. They'd never been separated before.

'And I'll miss you,' Iris said, 'but I won't be far away and we'll meet up every chance we get. One day you'll be training as a nurse too and maybe we'll both work in the same hospital!'

'Mmm,' Beth said. But she knew in her heart she didn't have the same passion to be a nurse that Iris did.

The day Iris started her training was the same day Miss Nightingale, her staff and cats, as well as Beth and George, set off for the Nightingale family home in Derbyshire.

Beth was amazed to find they had a whole carriage just to themselves on the train. The cats were all in wicker baskets and Scamp did not like that at all. He *miaow*ed and *miaow*ed to let everyone know he wasn't happy and eventually Beth let him out so he could sit on her lap instead. Once everyone was on board and settled, Florence said Tom, Topsy, Gladstone, Soyer, Aggy, Dickens, Izzy and Mr Bismarck could come out of their baskets too.

'Just watch the door and windows. We don't want anyone escaping!'

George's mother handed round the cakes and sandwiches she'd made and the cats tucked into tasty morsels of chicken.

It was afternoon by the time they arrived at Whatstandwell Station in Derbyshire.

'The fuzz-buzz said I walked to Lea Hurst from this station along the Cromford Canal carrying a heavy suitcase after my return from the Crimean War,' Florence said as George and Beth helped her off the train. 'But it isn't true. I really didn't want any publicity and I was glad when Lady Auckland met me at the station and took me home in her carriage. Although I have walked the route many times in the past and wish I could still do so. I'm not strong enough now and I wasn't then.'

'I'd like to walk it,' Beth said. It had been a long train journey and a stroll in the sunshine would be perfect.

'Then you must,' Miss Nightingale told her.

As Beth and George walked along the canal with Scamp trotting along beside them, making sure he didn't get too close to the swans, Beth breathed in the fresh country air. Around them there were wild flowers in bloom and animals in the fields. She didn't tell George she'd never seen a real-life cow before when he pointed to some grazing in a field.

'I never knew they'd be so big or have such gentle eyes,' she said. She couldn't wait to draw them, as well as the blue dragonflies she spotted dancing among the flowers. She wanted to draw everything and capture it in her sketchbook forever.

'There it is!' George said, pointing to a gabled stone manor house just visible among the trees.

'It's beautiful,' Beth said.

Lea Hurst was quite different from Miss Nightingale's London townhouse and much much bigger.

On entering the building, she found Miss Nightingale in the library that overlooked the lawns.

'Have you seen this book, Beth? Mister Darwin went far away to the Galapagos Islands to draw and write about the animals and plants he found there,' the lady said.

Beth shook her head as she remembered how awestruck she'd been when she'd met the famous naturalist at the Crystal Palace cat show. How remarkable that Scamp had helped her to meet so many wonderful people!

Florence handed her a copy of *The Voyage of the Beagle* and Beth curled up in a chair with Scamp beside her and pored over the book. She was fascinated by the illustrations inside it from the detailed lizard at the front to the different types of finch beaks in the middle. But it was what she read at the back of the book that made her gasp: '*In conclusion it appears to be that nothing can be more improving to a young naturalist, than a journey in different countries . . .*'

Florence looked over at her and smiled.

'Oh, I should so love to travel abroad one day,' Beth said, and she turned back to the book.

'I know you would,' Florence said as she picked up her pen and continued with the letter she was now writing.

*

The next day there was a letter for Beth from Iris.

It's very strict and we all must be most proper at all times. We wake up early and fall asleep full of learning. But I'm so pleased to be here, sometimes I have to pinch myself or I'd think it was all some marvellous dream and not real at all.

Miss Nightingale spent a lot of the time at Lea Hurst with her very elderly mother and father. But she also made time to sit outside with a protective straw hat on and watch while Beth sketched the kittens and cats playing on the lawn. Tom and Topsy loved racing around the grass together, Gladstone and Izzy liked to watch the birds, Aggy, Scamp and Dickens went off exploring whenever they got the chance, with Soyer, often as not, following along behind them.

'I've always loved animals ever since I was a child,' Florence said. 'And people. I've always wanted to do my best for them too. The local medical man, Doctor Dunn, and I have been planning how best to provide healthcare for the tenants that live in the Lea Hurst cottages. I will fund it and he will administer it. When we return to London the doctor's going to keep me informed of its progress. As well as making sure everyone has sufficient nutritious food, there will be free hospital stays, medicine and cleaning care.'

'You're so kind, Miss Nightingale,' Beth said.

'Oh, pish-posh,' the great lady told her. 'Come and see the shell collection I kept as a child.'

Scamp followed them as they went up the stairs.

Miss Nightingale had a bedroom and an adjoining sitting room with a large balcony. Beth was sharing a room with Hazel and Rose.

Each of Florence's shells was carefully labelled with details of when and where she had found it.

'Everyone has something inside themselves they know they are supposed to do,' she said as Beth inspected the shells. 'A purpose. Something that makes them feel alive, to lose track of time while they're doing it. Something really worthwhile.'

Beth nodded because she understood exactly what Florence meant.

'I think we both know there's something worthwhile that makes *your* heart sing, Beth' the lady said.

'Drawing,' Beth whispered.

Florence nodded. 'The detail in your work is impeccable,' she said. 'Many people have a talent, but yours, yours has the keen eye of the scientist about it too.'

Beth smiled and blushed.

'I've heard the Finsbury School of Art is really quite excellent and has produced some fine draughtswomen. You'll need to be very accurate for expedition work, you know, Beth. It isn't just about painting pretty pictures. It's about recording the finest of detail.'

'I know,' Beth said. It was one of the reasons she wanted to do it so badly.

'In the meantime, some naturalist friends of mine are off on a small expedition of their own shortly and I wondered if you would like to accompany them? They have a daughter about your age and she'll be going along too, so you would have a friend.'

Beth was already nodding her head very fast, eyes shining. 'I'd like that very much indeed, Miss Nightingale,' she said.

'This expedition is only round the British Isles and won't take you to the exotic places that future ones hopefully will. In fact, it's only for a few weeks, but I hope you will find ample opportunity to practise your draughtsmanship before you start at Finsbury School of Art in the autumn,' Miss Nightingale said as they headed back downstairs for tea.

Beth felt like pinching herself to make sure it wasn't all some wonderful dream. She was so happy she thought she'd never stop smiling. A *real* expedition and she was going on it!

'I don't know what you want to go off exploring anywhere else for when there's quite enough happening here!' George told Beth in a loud voice when he heard she was going on a boat with some of Miss Nightingale's friends.

'Don't you, George?' asked Miss Nightingale. 'That's a shame because I was hoping you might like to accompany Beth. But if you don't want to, I'm sure I can find someone else.'

'Oh, I do want to,' George said quickly.

'Good, because I'd like her to have her trusty bodyguard with her.' Florence smiled mischievously at Beth.

Beth hugged Scamp. She was going to miss him terribly. Ever since they'd come here he'd slept on her pillow every night. Fortunately, Rose and Hazel who shared the bedroom were cat lovers too.

'It won't be for long, Scamp,' she whispered into his soft fluffy fur.

A few days later, Scamp was sitting on the windowsill in Miss Nightingale's bedroom watching the birds pecking crumbs on the balcony when Beth came running into the room holding a carpetbag.

'It's almost time to go,' she said breathlessly, dropping the bag on the floor. 'George is sitting in the coach.'

'He's already been to say goodbye,' Florence told her.

Scamp hopped off the windowsill and looked at the open carpetbag full of soft clothes lying so invitingly on the floor. Neither Beth nor Florence noticed as he climbed inside, raked at the clothes to make himself a nest to sleep in and snuggled down.

'I want the promise of a letter or two and maybe even a drawing every now and again so I know how you're getting on,' Miss Nightingale said to Beth.

'I'll send hundreds of letters!' Beth promised. She'd already written to Iris telling her the good news and promising to write to her every day too. Although there was going to be so much to see she wasn't sure she'd have time to write more than a few lines. There was the prospect of fossils from dinosaurs at Lyme Regis, and a visit to the Isle of Skye and the Outer Hebrides, as well as the Channel Islands of Guernsey, Jersey, Sark and Herm, where she hoped to find the perfect shell for Florence on the beach. She wasn't even sure if she'd have enough sketchbooks to draw everything.

'One letter a week will do,' said Miss Nightingale. 'I want you to have time for fun too! Oh, and I thought you could make use of this. Apparently Vicky has one just like it.'

She pointed to a canvas artist's bag containing not only a range of soft and hard grey lead pencils and a sketchbook, but also a set of beautiful watercolour paints.

'Oh, thank you!' Beth said, and she threw her arms round Florence and gave her a hug.

She lifted the precious artist's bag over her shoulder, picked up her carpetbag and ran down the stairs to the waiting carriage. George was already sitting inside.

'What took you so l–' he started to say when they both heard a *miaow* coming from Beth's luggage.

'What are *you* doing in there?' Beth laughed as she lifted Scamp out. 'You can't come on the expedition too, you know.'

But when she took Scamp back to Miss Nightingale, the lady had other ideas.

'He'll never be happy here without you, you know, Beth. I took my owl Athena with me on the Grand Tour of Europe with much success,' she said. 'But don't forget to take Scamp's reins with you and make sure he wears them on board the ship!'

Beth grinned and returned to the coach with Scamp and his ribbon harness and lead.

'He's coming with us!' she told a surprised George.

'Good!' he laughed. 'I've always thought Scamp looked like a seafaring pirate cat with that patch of black fur over his eye.'

Edward dropped them at Whatstandwell Station and they caught the train to Liverpool where Miss Nightingale's friends were to meet them on the platform.

'My mother made us lots of grub for the journey,' George said, opening the food bag almost as soon as the train left the station. Some of the sandwiches had potted chicken in them, which Scamp liked very much.

After a few hours and a long nap for Scamp, they arrived at Liverpool Lime Street Station.

'I'll bring the bags,' George said as Beth carried Scamp off the train.

The little calico kitten gazed up at the pigeons flying about the rafters, but Beth stared straight ahead in amazement as she saw who was coming towards her along the platform. It was the girl from Hyde Park, a King Charles spaniel puppy bounding along beside her. They were accompanied by a tall, friendly-looking man and a woman.

'Maude!' Beth cried happily.

'Oh, there you are!' Maude exclaimed, her face grinning with delight. 'We've been waiting ages. Hello, Scamp – Oscar's going to be very pleased to have a friend to play with on our trip!'

Scamp looked down at Oscar from Beth's arms and gave a little *miaow*.

Then George came over with the bags.

'Hello, George, I'm glad you're coming too,' Maude said.

George looked amazed to see her and his mouth dropped open. 'We know you!'

'Did you bring your fishing gear? George is very handy with a line,' Maude told her parents with a smile.

'No space to bring it,' George said sadly.

'Not to worry, we'll lend you one!' Maude's father told him as they headed to the docks.

Beth found a letter from Miss Nightingale waiting for her in her berth.

My dear Beth,
I'm delighted that you are setting off on a voyage of adventure and give thanks indeed for the day we first met. Write soon, my dear.
Your friend,
Florence Nightingale

'Miss Nightingale is so kind and thoughtful!' Beth told Scamp, who was looking very comfortable already curled up on her pillow.

She hoped the lady would be pleased with the drawing she had left in the library that morning. It was of her cats playing on the lawn; she'd only just finished it, along with a letter thanking Miss Nightingale for all she'd done for her and Iris, before they'd had to leave.

Outside on the deck, Beth could hear George and Maude laughing and Oscar yapping his high puppy bark. It was a glorious day for an expedition to start.

Scamp looked up at Beth with his big amber eyes and gave a *miaow* as they went to join them.

Glossary

Agnes Elizabeth Jones (10 November 1832–February 1868): a nurse who trained at the Nightingale School at St Thomas's Hospital in London in 1862. She became the first trained nursing superintendent of the Liverpool Workhouse Infirmary. Florence Nightingale said of her, 'She overworked as others underworked.'

Alexis Benoit Soyer (4 February 1810– 5 August 1858): a French chef who invented the travelling stove, which was lightweight and easy to carry, for working in remote places, such as field hospitals. In 1855 he went to the Crimea to help with cooking for the army. He also wrote many cookery books, including *Instructions for Military Hospitals* (1860).

Bryant and May: a British company set up by William Bryant and Francis May to make matches; the original factory was in Bow, east London, close to the River Lea, and was the site of the London Match Girls' Strike in 1888, which was came about through bad working conditions and pay.

Charles John Huffam Dickens (7 February 1812–9 June 1870): a famous English author who wrote powerful stories describing life in Victorian times, featuring many unforgettable characters. *A Christmas Carol*, *Oliver Twist* and *Great Expectations* are just some of his well-known books.

Charles Robert Darwin (12 February 1809–19 April 1882): an English naturalist who shocked Victorian society with his theory of evolution, which suggested that animals and humans shared a common ancestry. After returning from a fact-finding voyage round the world aboard HMS *Beagle*, he wrote *On the Origin of Species* (1859).

cholera: a disease caused by consuming infected food or water.

Crimean War, the (1853–1856): a major European conflict of the 1800s. Britain, France, Turkey and Sardinia fought against Russia on the Crimean peninsula, and also on the Black Sea. Britain and France entered the war in 1854. Florence Nightingale heard about the terrible conditions and went out there to help nurse wounded soldiers.

Crystal Palace cat show, the: the world's first cat show, held at the Crystal Palace in

Hyde Park, London, in July 1871. It was organized by Harrison Weir, an English gentleman and natural history artist. Many new breeds of cat were on display, and 200,000 guests are said to have visited. The magnificent cast-iron and plate-glass building had originally housed the Great Exhibition of 1851.

East End, the: a poor area of London to the east of the City.

Education Act of 1870, the: the first of a number of Acts of Parliament that made education in England and Wales compulsory for children aged between five and twelve.

Florence Nightingale (12 May 1820–13 August 1910): known as the lady with the lamp, Florence became famous as the founder of modern nursing. When news reached England that soldiers fighting in the Crimean War were dying in terrible conditions, she travelled out there with a team of nurses to help. Together they worked to provide better equipment, better food and cleaner surroundings to stop the spread of disease.

Florence Nightingale's cats: when Florence returned from the Crimea, her health was never the same. However, she spent a lot of time writing books and pamphlets at home, surrounded by pet cats that were named after well-known people of the time. It is said that her favourite was a Persian called Mr Bismarck.

Frances Parthenope Nightingale (19 April 1819–12 May 1890): known as Parthe, Frances was the elder sister of Florence. She married Harry Verney of Claydon House, Buckinghamshire, in 1858, and was a great supporter of her sister's work.

Isambard Kingdom Brunel (9 April 1806–15 September 1859): a famous British engineer who designed tunnels, bridges, railway lines and ships, including the iron-hulled steamship *Great Britain* (1843), which can still be seen today in Bristol docks. In 1855 he also designed a prefabricated hospital building that was sent over to the Crimea in pieces, then fitted together on arrival.

Lea Hurst: the childhood home of Florence Nightingale, near Matlock, in north Derbyshire.

Mary Seacole (23 November 1805–14 May 1881): the daughter of a Jamaican mother and a Scottish soldier, Mary became a nurse and heroine of the Crimean War. In 1854 she set up the British Hotel near Balaclava to look after sick and wounded officers. She also nursed injured soldiers on the battlefield, sometimes under fire.

Match tax of 1871, the: a tax on matches proposed by the government. The workers at Bryant and May realized this threatened their jobs and marched to the House of Commons in London to protest on 24 April 1871. The tax was never imposed.

Nightingale School of Nursing: a training school for nurses that was set up at St Thomas's Hospital, London, on the banks of the River Thames. Inspired by the work of Florence Nightingale and her team during the Crimean War, in 1855 a fund was set up by members of the public to pay for it. The first nurses began their training on 9 July 1860 and were known as Nightingales.

***Notes on Nursing: What It Is, and What It Is Not*:** a book by Florence Nightingale, first published in 1859. It contained sensible advice for those entrusted with caring for the health of others, including hints on heating, noise, light, bedding and cleanliness.

number 10 South Street, Mayfair, London: the house that Florence Nightingale moved into in 1865 when she was forty-five years old, and where she died in 1910 at the age of ninety.

Otto von Bismarck (1 April 1815–30 July 1898): a German politician who became known as the Iron Chancellor, Bismarck ruled the state of Prussia, then, in 1871, became the first chancellor of the new, unified nation of Germany.

Palace of Westminster: the seat of the two houses of the Parliament of the United Kingdom: the House of Commons and the House of Lords.

Peelers: a name for police officers, after the home secretary Sir Robert Peel passed the Metropolitan Police Act in 1829, providing full-time constables to protect the London area as part of the Metropolitan Police Force.

phossy jaw: a disease suffered by those who worked with white phosphorus, especially in the matchstick industry in Victorian times. The symptoms included painful toothache, swelling of the gums and damage to the jawbone.

Thomas John Barnardo (4 July 1845–19 September 1905): an Irishman who came over to London to train as a doctor. Shocked by the awful conditions of those living on the streets, he decided to help. He set up his first 'ragged school' in 1867 in the East End to teach poor orphans. By the time he died in 1905 his homes and schools were caring for over 8,000 children.

typhus fever: a disease spread by lice, fleas or mites in overcrowded and dirty conditions.

William Ewart Gladstone (29 December 1809–19 May 1898): a famous politician of the Victorian era who was prime minister of the United Kingdom four times between 1868 and 1894.

Acknowledgements

Florence and the Mischievous Kitten has been an absolute joy to write, from the wonderful discovery that the amazing lady with the lamp was also a cat lover, to learning what a maths whizz she was.

As always I've been fortunate to have worked with some extremely talented people in the production of this book, especially my editor Emma Jones, copy-editors Stephanie Barrett and Mary O'Riordan and proofreader Jennie Roman. The beautiful cover and chapter heading illustrations are thanks to Angelo Rinaldi and Dominica Clements. On the PR and marketing side I'm looking forward to working with Ellen Grady and Beth O'Brien, and once again sales experts Kat Baker and Lexy Mennie have worked their magic.

My agent and friend Clare Pearson continues to help steer my writing career with wise insight.

I was just starting my research for the story when I was invited to Stockton-on-Tees for the twenty-first anniversary of the Stockton Children's Book of the Year Award – which *The Victory Dogs* won back in 2014. Lucy Carlton-Walker and the Stockton library service were extremely helpful and supportive as always, and Lizzie Prediger and Ivan Limon had lots of funny cat stories to tell me, which I haven't used yet but may do one day . . .

Most of the book was written while I was recovering from a broken shoulder (humerus – four places). My dogs, golden retrievers Bella and Freya, often come into schools and to festivals with me to demonstrate ways in which assistance dogs help people, and they certainly helped *me* by picking up and bringing items to me during this time – as well as being endlessly available for cuddles. My husband Eric was amazing throughout as always, and made so many delicious meals I thought he should be on Masterchef. Thankfully I'm now fully recovered and about to start Level 2 of British Sign Language. I hope to do more signing presentations in the near future.

I truly hope that I have done a little in this book to show how awe-inspiring, generous, funny and determined Florence Nightingale was. As she said:

'Live life while you have it. Life is a splendid gift – there is nothing small about it.'

Turn the page for an extract from

Emmeline and the Plucky Pup

by Megan Rix

AVAILABLE NOW

www.meganrix.com

Prologue

1906

'Alfie, Alfie, wake up!' a voice hissed into the darkness.

Half asleep, Alfie pulled the threadbare blanket over his head and wriggled down further in his lumpy bed. Around him in the dormitory, another hundred boys snored and snuffled as they slept, tired out from the long workhouse day. They were woken at six o'clock in the morning, did lessons till noon and then worked all afternoon, with only gruel and watery stew or bread for each meal, and went to bed at eight o'clock. Usually work meant putting the heads on pins, or breaking stones into little bits. Sometimes Alfie folded sheets that had been pressed by the mangle in the laundry and once he'd helped to peel hundreds and hundreds of potatoes. But this afternoon he'd been given a new, much more fun job.

'Alfie, take Sniffer for a walk,' Matron had said.

'Me?' Alfie wasn't used to dogs and had never walked one before. He'd looked down at Matron's elderly Yorkshire terrier, which could be very growly at people he wasn't fond of.

The two of them set off round the workhouse yard, with Alfie gently holding Sniffer's lead. This afternoon Sniffer didn't growl even once.

'Sniffer does seem to like you,' Matron said, as Sniffer rolled over on to his back and Alfie gave him a tummy rub. 'And he doesn't like many people, as you know.'

Alfie liked Sniffer too and hoped he could take him for another walk in the morning.

'Alfie – it's me!' A hand shook his shoulder and gave him a gentle flick on his sleepy shaved head.

Only one person flicked him like that.

Alfie's eyes flew open. 'What are you doing here, Daisy?' he whispered into the darkness. 'You'll be for it if you're caught.'

'Get up.' His big sister pulled the blanket from his bed.

It was freezing in the dormitory and Alfie had put all his day clothes back on over his nightshirt for warmth, even though he knew how much trouble he'd be in if Matron caught him wearing them. Daisy was wearing her grey workhouse dress and long white apron.

'You shouldn't be h–' he said.

Daisy pressed her finger to his lips.

'*Shush!* We're leaving. Right now.'

Alfie gulped. They couldn't just leave the workhouse, not without permission. What if Matron or the governor or the police caught them? They could be sent to prison or brought back to the workhouse and punished. Alfie didn't want to be locked in a little room by himself or beaten with a stick, and he certainly didn't want to be given less food to eat. There was barely enough to stop his belly from rumbling as it was.

'Come on.' Daisy grabbed his wrist and pulled him up.

'We could get sent to prison . . .'

'Sssh!'

Alfie pushed his bare feet into his wooden clogs and wrapped the blanket around his skinny shoulders. He didn't have a coat and he wasn't leaving the blanket behind, even though all of the boys in the dormitory knew what had happened to the other boys who'd tried to escape and been caught by the police. Not only had those boys been sent to prison but they were given even longer prison sentences because they'd dared to escape wearing *stolen* workhouse clothes.

Daisy was already making her way soundlessly past the sleeping boys, some of them crammed two or three to a narrow bed. Alfie tried to catch up with her, but one of his clogs slipped off and landed with a *clonk* on the floor. He froze with fear. The noise must have woken someone up! They'd be caught and then . . . well, Alfie didn't like to think about that.

Daisy crept back to him, picked up his clog, then took off the one that was on his other foot. She put her finger to her lips and tiptoed to the dormitory door, with Alfie creeping after her. He was so scared he had to put his hands over his mouth to stop his teeth from chattering.

Daisy had left her own clogs in the corridor outside. She picked them up but didn't put them back on. Alfie's feet were freezing. They made little slapping sounds on the stone floor as he ran after his sister.

He'd often seen Daisy and the other girls on their hands and knees scrubbing the long corridors with hard brushes and soapy water. Matron said it had to be done every day to keep the dirt away. She didn't like dirt. It was why he'd had to have his head shaved. 'Fleas and sneezes spread diseases,' she'd told him, as he watched locks of his dark hair landing on the floor and a small girl quickly gathered them up.

There were lots of sneezes and diseases at the workhouse, as well as fleas.

The stairs were just ahead of them. Downstairs was the room where Matron slept, with her name written on the door. Alfie stopped at the top of the stairs but Daisy took his hand and squeezed it.

'We have to,' she whispered.

The moon was shining through the big window on the landing and he saw that she looked as frightened as he felt.

He looked back along the corridor. Maybe they should go back? Daisy squeezed his hand again.

Alfie nodded but dared not speak. He held on to the polished wooden bannister and stepped as softly as he could. At the bottom he tiptoed across the tiled entrance hall after Daisy.

They were nearly past Matron's door when a dog started yapping and Alfie almost jumped out of his skin.

Sniffer!

The yapping was followed by a great hacking, heaving cough from inside the room.

People were always getting sick at the workhouse. Some of them, like Alfie's mum, didn't get better and died from it. Now it sounded like Matron was sick too. But she was also awake!

Sniffer barked again, then he whined and Alfie heard the little dog scratching at the door.

Daisy grabbed Alfie's arm and dragged him down a corridor leading to the dining hall and kitchens. She stopped so suddenly Alfie bumped into her.

'This way,' she said, pushing up a sash window and climbing out.

After a quick look behind him, Alfie followed her.

Now they were in the yard where Alfie had taken Sniffer for a walk that afternoon. He'd never been out here at night and he moved closer to Daisy. Why had she brought him here? It wasn't safe. The yard was surrounded on three sides by red brick walls. Alfie stared up at them. Had they been seen from one of the windows? Was someone standing there looking out? Or maybe someone was already on their way, running down the stairs to drag them back.

Alfie pulled his blanket over his head to hide his face.

In the fourth wall were the massive wooden gates of the workhouse. They were guarded day and night by a fierce man with a big stick. He lived in a little hut next to the gates. What if he came out? What if he caught them? Alfie didn't want the gatekeeper to swing his stick at him or Daisy.

'Stay in the shadows,' Daisy told him, as they edged their way round the yard until they came to a small side door.

She pulled a large key from the pocket of her apron, turned it in the lock, swiftly lifted the latch, and the next moment they were out in the street.

Alfie looked at the workhouse behind him. They were out. Really out. He'd been at the Manchester workhouse since he was three and never been out of it before at night. He swallowed hard and tried not to think about what would happen if they were caught.

Daisy pulled a screwed-up piece of paper from her apron pocket.

'What's that?' Alfie asked.

'A map,' she told him, as she peered at it under a gas light.

'To where?'

'To Mrs Pankhurst's.'

'Who's Mrs Pankhurst?'

But Daisy didn't answer. She put the map back in her pocket and pointed to the tall iron gates across the cobbled street.

Alfie gasped. 'Not the cemetery! We can't go in there.'

'You're not scared?' Daisy hissed scornfully. 'We've got a lot more to be frightened of from real-life living people than from any ghosts!'

But Alfie *was* scared and he really didn't want to go into the cemetery – especially not at night. A drop of rain landed on his face and then one fell on his hand. He hoped the rain would keep the cemetery ghosts away.

'If the workhouse gatekeeper comes looking for us, he won't think to look in there, will he?' Daisy said. 'The cemetery's not that big – if we run as fast as we can, we'll be through it in no time. Here, I'll hold your hand.'

Alfie sighed and squeezed through a gap in the padlocked gates after Daisy.

'Run!'

It wasn't easy running in clogs but Alfie moved so fast they didn't have a chance to slip off. He was gasping so hard it felt like his heart was going to burst by the time they reached the other gate.

Daisy clutched her stomach and leant over, drawing in big breaths of freezing night air.

An owl hooted as it flew overhead and they both jumped in fear and then laughed with relief.

'Just an owl.'

'Now where?' Alfie asked Daisy.

'Down Nell Lane,' she said, peering at her map, although Alfie didn't think she could see it properly now it was drizzling with rain.

They headed down Nell Lane and then along the banks of Chorlton Brook, where there were no street lamps and it was very dark.

Alfie's feet and legs were soon soaked in the long wet grass.

'Is it much further to Mrs Pankhurst's?' he wanted to know when they reached Sandy Lane. 'These clogs are rubbing the skin off my feet.'

They'd been walking for over an hour.

'This is the quickest way,' Daisy told him, as they headed into Ivy Green woods. 'One of the old ladies, Mary Dingle, drew the map to Mrs Pankhurst's house for me. She said we should always keep the river Mersey on our left.'

Alfie listened for the sound of running water. He couldn't swim and he didn't want to end up in the river!

Suddenly he heard someone groaning and icy fingers of terror ran down his spine.

'Daisy –' he started to say.

Daisy let out a great scream as a cow came running out of the bushes straight for her.

Not groaning but lowing!

The cow stopped dead and stared at them with its huge eyes. Alfie had never been close to a cow before but he wasn't frightened. He went to stroke it but the cow backed off and then turned the other way.

'I wasn't really scared,' Daisy said, as they headed onwards.

'I know,' Alfie told her.

Soon they'd left the countryside behind and were back on the cobblestone streets. It started to rain more heavily and Alfie and Daisy huddled together under the workhouse blanket, but they were soaked through in no time.

Just as Alfie was thinking he couldn't go any further, Daisy turned into a wide street lined with dark houses. Alfie caught a glimpse of the sign: Nelson Street. Daisy pulled him along faster, peering urgently at the house numbers, until finally they stopped at number 62. Daisy marched up to the front door and pulled on the brass bell pull.